First day disaster

Mrs. Brisbane opened the classroom door and soon, students started to come in.

I realized right away that something was wrong. *Terribly* wrong.

Mrs. Brisbane smiled as the students entered.

"Take a seat," she said. "Any seat."

I climbed up high in my cage to get a better look.

"Who are these kids, Og?" I asked my neighbor. "I've never seen any of them before!"

"BOING!" he answered, splashing noisily.

More unfamiliar students came into the room. One of them was a girl who whizzed by in her wheelchair. Another was a boy who was really tall. He was as tall as our teacher—maybe taller!

"Just take a seat, children." How could Mrs. Brisbane sound so cheery, knowing these students didn't belong in Room 26?

As the classroom hamster, I felt I had to squeak up.

"You're in the wrong room!" I squeaked. "This is not your room, go back!"

READ ALL OF HUMPHREY'S ADVENTURES!

NONFICTION BOOKS
FEATURING HUMPHREY

HUMPHREY'S TINY TALES
FOR YOUNG READERS

School Days according to Humphrey

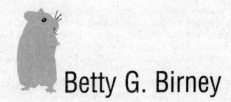

Betty G. Birney

PUFFIN BOOKS
An Imprint of Penguin Group (USA)

PUFFIN BOOKS
Published by the Penguin Group
Penguin Group (USA) LLC
375 Hudson Street
New York, New York 10014

USA • Canada • UK • Ireland • Australia
New Zealand • India • South Africa • China

penguin.com
A Penguin Random House Company

First published in the United States of America by G. P. Putnam's Sons,
a division of Penguin Young Readers Group, 2011
Published by Puffin Books, a division of Penguin Young Readers Group, 2012

THE LIBRARY OF CONGRESS HAS CATALOGED THE G. P. PUTNAM'S SONS EDITION AS FOLLOWS:
Birney, Betty G.
School days according to Humphrey / Betty G. Birney.
p. cm.
Summary: Humphrey the hamster is puzzled when unfamiliar students fill Mrs. Brisbane's
classroom at summer's end, but he soon learns that his friends from last year are fine
and that the new class needs his special help.
ISBN: 978-0-399-25413-0 (hc)
[1. Schools—Fiction. 2. Hamsters—Fiction. 3. Frogs—Fiction. 4. Friendship—Fiction.]
I. Title.
PZ7.B52285Fr 2011
[Fic]—dc22 2010014792

Puffin Books ISBN 978-0-14-242106-2

Printed in the United States of America

To Humphrey's unsqueakably
faithful fans everywhere.

And special thanks to Rita de Leeuw for her
invaluable assistance with this book.

Contents

The Worst First Day Begins

I t was a quiet morning in Room 26, so quiet that all I could hear was the SCRATCH-SCRATCH-SCRATCH-ing of my pencil as I wrote in my little notebook.

"I'm writing a poem about the end of summer, Og," I squeaked to my neighbor, the classroom frog. (I am Humphrey, the classroom hamster.) "I'll read you what I have so far."

> *Summer, oh, summer,*
> *I hate to say good-bye.*
> *Summer, oh, summer,*
> *Must you end . . . and why?*

Og splashed gently in his tank as I continued.

> *I loved summer days*
> *At Camp Happy Hollow.*
> *And now that they're over . . .*

I stopped because there was nothing more to read. "BOING?" Og twanged. Green frogs like him don't say "ribbit." They make a sound like a broken guitar string. "BOING-BOING!"

"I haven't finished it yet, Og," I explained. "I have to find a word that rhymes with *hollow. Wallow?* Or *swallow?*"

I stared down at the page again.

> *I loved summer days*
> *At Camp Happy Hollow.*
> *And now that they're over,*
> *I can hardly swallow!*

Og dived down deeply in his tank, splashing noisily.

"I don't think much of that line, either," I replied. "I'll try again."

Just then, our teacher, Mrs. Brisbane, came bustling into the room, carrying a stack of papers. As usual, I quickly hid my notebook behind the mirror in my cage. As much as I love humans, some things are better kept private.

"After all my years of teaching, I should have known by now that on the first day of school, the line for the copy machine would be out the door," Mrs. Brisbane said.

She stacked the papers on her desk and stared up at the chalkboard and the bulletin boards, which were bare, except for a list of rules in Mrs. Brisbane's neat printing.

I'd copied those rules in my notebook while Mrs. Brisbane was down at the office and I intended to memorize them as soon as possible.

Mrs. Brisbane glanced up at the clock. "School will

start soon," she said, turning toward the table by the window where Og and I spend most of our time. "In case you two are interested."

"I am!" I said, and I meant it.

Even though I was sorry that summer was ending, I was GLAD-GLAD-GLAD to be back in good old Room 26 again. After the last camp session was over, my friend Ms. Mac brought me back to the house where Mrs. Brisbane and her husband, Bert, live. Og and I spent a few weeks with them.

I love to go to the Brisbanes' house, but it was so quiet there, I was looking forward to seeing my classmates again. Some of them had been at camp, like A.J., Garth, Miranda and Sayeh. But I hadn't seen some of the others for an unsqueakably long time!

The door swung open and in walked the Most Important Person at Longfellow School, Principal Morales. Mrs. Brisbane is in charge of a whole class of students, but Mr. Morales is in charge of the whole school.

As usual, he was wearing an interesting tie. This one had little books in many different colors.

"Morning, Sue," he said to Mrs. Brisbane. "Ready to go?"

"As ready as I'll ever be," she said.

He walked over to our table by the window. "Guys, I hope you're all set to go back to work."

"YES-YES-YES," I answered, wishing that he could hear more than just the usual "SQUEAK-SQUEAK-SQUEAK" humans hear.

3

"BOING!" Og agreed.

"Good," the principal said, glancing up at the clock. "I'd better be outside to meet the buses. Have a great one, Sue."

"You too," Mrs. Brisbane said.

She hurried back to her desk and studied a piece of paper, then began muttering strange words like "feebee-harrykelsey."

Goodness, were we going to be learning a new language this year?

"Thomasrosiepaul."

Did she say *Paul*? I knew that word. It was the name of a boy who had come into our class for math last year.

I was about to point this out to Og when the bell rang as loud as ever. No matter how long I'm a student in Room 26, I'll never get used to that noisy bell.

Mrs. Brisbane opened the classroom door and soon, students started to come in.

I realized right away that something was wrong. *Terribly* wrong.

Mrs. Brisbane smiled as the students entered.

"Take a seat," she said. "Any seat."

I climbed up high in my cage to get a better look.

"Who are these kids, Og?" I asked my neighbor. "I've never seen any of them before!"

"BOING!" he answered, splashing noisily.

More unfamiliar students came into the room. One of them was a girl who whizzed by in her wheelchair.

Another was a boy who was really tall. He was as tall as our teacher—maybe taller!

"Just take a seat, children." How could Mrs. Brisbane sound so cheery, knowing these students didn't belong in Room 26?

As the classroom hamster, I felt I had to squeak up.

"You're in the wrong room!" I squeaked. "This is not your room, go back!"

"Welcome," Mrs. Brisbane told the students. "Take a seat."

"Wrong room!" I scrambled to the tippy top of my cage. "This is Room Twenty-six!"

Unfortunately, my voice is small and squeaky and I guess nobody heard me, because the students went ahead and sat down.

Mrs. Brisbane kept on smiling and nobody budged. Oh, how I wished I had a loud voice like my old friend Lower-Your-Voice-A.J.

When the bell rang again, my heart sank. Mrs. Brisbane is a GREAT-GREAT-GREAT teacher and pretty smart for a human. Why didn't she notice that her class was full of the wrong students?

"Og? What should we do?" I asked my froggy friend.

This time he didn't answer. I guess he was as confused as I was.

"Hey, Humphrey! It's me! Hi!" a familiar voice shouted.

Slow-Down-Simon raced up to my cage. He was the younger brother of Stop-Giggling-Gail Morgenstern, who *did* belong in Room 26. But she was nowhere in sight.

"Now *I'll* get to take you home some weekend," Simon announced.

"Go back to your own room or you'll be late!" I warned him.

Mrs. Brisbane told him to take a seat. Simon twirled around and rushed away, bumping right into a girl with bright red hair whose chair was sticking out in the aisle.

"You should be more careful, Kelsey," he said.

"*You* ran into me!" The girl rubbed her arm. She probably got a big bruise. Ouch!

"What's happening just doesn't make sense!" I told Og. I don't think I was making a lot of sense, either. It was as if the world had just been turned all upside down and Og and I were the only ones who noticed.

"Hi, Humphrey," a soft voice said.

I looked up and there was Paul Fletcher, whom I thought of as Small-Paul. He was the boy who came in for math class every day last year because he was unsqueakably good with numbers.

Paul was smart. I knew he'd understand.

"Why are these students in the wrong room?" I asked him.

He pushed up his glasses, which had slid down his nose. "This year I get to take you home," he said. "I can't wait!"

What was he talking about? Only students in Room 26 got to take me home for the weekend.

"Settle down, class," Mrs. Brisbane said. "Please take your seats."

Class? What was she talking about? This wasn't my class. Where were A.J. and Garth, Heidi and Mandy? Where were Gail and her giggles? Where were Richie, Art, Tabitha and Seth? Where were Kirk and his jokes? And where in the world was the almost perfect Golden-Miranda?

"Mrs. Brisbane?" I squeaked. "In case you haven't noticed, *this isn't our class*!"

Mrs. Brisbane was too busy counting the students to hear me.

"We're short one student," she said. "But while we're waiting, let me welcome you all to Room Twenty-six!"

Crushed, I scrambled back down to the floor of my cage and scurried into my sleeping hut, where I could be alone and think.

I remembered that poem I'd just written about summer. Now I had an idea for a new verse:

> *Summer, oh, summer,*
> *With days long and lazy.*
> *Now that you're over,*
> *Things are going crazy!*

HUMPHREY'S RULES OF SCHOOL: Before you take your seat in a classroom, it's always a good idea to make sure you're in the right room. This is important!

7

The Worst First Day Gets Worse

The final bell rang and everybody had taken a seat except the girl in a wheelchair, who was already sitting. There was still one empty chair left.

Mrs. Brisbane went to the door and looked out into the hall.

"Oh, there you are," she said.

She opened the door wider and a boy walked in.

"You must be the missing student," Mrs. Brisbane said.

"I'm not missing," the boy answered. "I'm right here."

I thought he'd be in big trouble, so I was surprised when Mrs. Brisbane smiled and directed him to the empty chair. Then she stood in the front of the class.

"Good morning, class," Mrs. Brisbane said. "Last year, I had one of the best classes ever. But I think this class will be even better!"

"Better?" I squeaked. "That was the BEST-BEST-BEST class in the whole wide world!"

"BOING-BOING!" Og agreed.

I wasn't sure what I said was true. On the one paw, I couldn't imagine a better class than the one we'd had last year. On the other paw, it was the only class I'd ever been in. But where had my classmates gone?

"I'm going to rearrange the seating later in the day," Mrs. Brisbane said. "But for now, I'll take attendance."

"Are you listening, Og?" I asked my neighbor. I can never be sure, because he doesn't have any ears that I've ever seen. But he seems to understand me most of the time.

"Are we dreaming?" I wondered. So far, the morning felt like one of those dreams where everything seems almost the same as in real life but a lot weirder. For instance, I once had a dream where all of my human friends were rolling around in giant hamster balls. That was a very funny dream.

Once I dreamed that the class was being taught by Mrs. Wright, the P.E. teacher. That wasn't a funny dream because she was always blowing on her very loud whistle, which is painful to the small, sensitive ears of a hamster.

Again, Og didn't answer me. Maybe frogs don't dream.

Then Mrs. Brisbane began to call out the strange words she had been saying before. It turns out they were names.

"Kelsey Kirkpatrick?"

"Here," the red-haired girl said, still rubbing her arm.

"Harry Ito?" Mrs. Brisbane called out.

Harry was the boy who had been late to class.

She called on Simon, who answered, "Present!"

Present? I didn't see any presents. Was it somebody's birthday?

"Rosie Rodriguez?" Mrs. Brisbane said.

The girl in the wheelchair waved her hand and shouted out, "Here!"

A boy named Thomas answered next, followed by a couple of girls, Phoebe and Holly.

"Are you paying attention, Og?" I asked my friend.

Og splashed a little but didn't answer.

And then something really odd happened.

"Paul?" Mrs. Brisbane asked.

Right away, not one but two voices replied, "Here."

One of them was Small-Paul from last year. The other Paul was the tall boy.

Mrs. Brisbane smiled. "I forgot. This year we have two Pauls in our class. Paul Fletcher and Paul Green. Now, how will we tell you apart?"

That was an easy question. One of them was SMALL-SMALL-SMALL and one of them was TALL-TALL-TALL.

Small-Paul and Tall-Paul eyed each other. Neither of them looked happy to have another Paul in the class.

"What did your teacher do last year?" she asked.

"He wasn't in my class," Small-Paul said.

"I went to another school," Tall-Paul added.

Mrs. Brisbane nodded. "I see. Do either of you have a nickname?"

Both boys shook their heads.

"Well, for now, let's say Paul F. and Paul G. Is that all right with you?" she asked.

Both boys nodded.

Then Mrs. Brisbane called out one more name. "Joseph?"

A boy with curly brown hair shifted in his chair a little but didn't answer.

Mrs. Brisbane looked around at the class. "Is Joseph here?"

The boy with curly brown hair nodded. "Yes, ma'am," he said. "But it's not Joseph. It's Joey. Just Joey Jones."

Mrs. Brisbane smiled. "All right, then. Just-Joey it is. Now, class, I'm very excited to get to know you and for you to get to know me. In case you don't know, I'm Mrs. Brisbane."

The teacher wrote her name on the board.

"There are two other members of the class you need to know," she said.

Then she wrote my name on the board. "Humphrey is our classroom hamster," she said.

Everybody—and I mean everybody—turned to look at me.

Next, she wrote Og's name on the board. "Og is our classroom frog. You'll get to know them both very well this year. You'll also have a chance to take Humphrey home for the weekend. I'll tell you more about that this afternoon," she said.

The students all giggled and whispered and turned in their seats to look at us.

"Tell them they're in the wrong room!" I suggested, and some of the students close to my cage giggled when they heard me go, "SQUEAK-SQUEAK-SQUEAK."

The teacher ignored me. "First, let's get to know each other a little better. Would you take out your summer boxes?"

"Summer boxes?" I squeaked. "What are they, Og?"

Summer was sunshine and campfires and unsqueakable fun. Summer wasn't something you could just put in a box.

I'm not sure Og could hear me since he was splashing like crazy in his tank. But the strange students in class seemed to understand. They reached into their backpacks and pulled out boxes—all kinds of boxes—and put them on their desks.

"How did they know about the boxes?" I squeaked to Og. "Why didn't we know?"

Og had no answer.

During the previous school year, I tried hard to keep up with my friends' homework, taking tests along with them, writing papers and even poems. Mrs. Brisbane didn't know I did the work, but I knew it, and that's what counts.

"All right, students. Let's share our summer experiences," Mrs. Brisbane said. "That way, I'll learn a little bit about all of you. And you'll learn about me, because I brought a box, too."

Mrs. Brisbane took a box out of a drawer and placed it on her desk.

"I'll tell you about my summer first," she said.

That got my attention. While I was at camp for the summer, Mrs. Brisbane was doing something else, but I still wasn't really sure *what*.

"My son lives in Tokyo, Japan," she said. "He's a teacher there. This summer, he got married, so my husband and I went to Japan for the wedding."

The smile on Mrs. Brisbane's face let me know that she'd had a GREAT-GREAT-GREAT time.

"Weddings in Japan are very beautiful," she said. "The couple dresses in traditional Japanese kimonos."

She held up a picture of a couple in very fancy clothes. "That's my son, Jason, and his new wife, Miki." Mrs. Brisbane sounded very proud.

She passed around some Japanese money for the students to see. Next, she took out a red plastic ball she'd bought in Tokyo. I couldn't see it very well.

"Something's inside, Og!" I scampered up to the top of my cage to get a better look.

"BOING!" he replied. I guess he couldn't see, either.

"I hope Humphrey won't be jealous," Mrs. Brisbane said. "Meet Aki."

She set the ball on the desk and the students howled with laughter as the ball started spinning wildly and colored lights flashed.

"Rockin' Aki!" a strange, loud voice wailed. "Rock 'n' roll rules!"

The ball looped and twirled unexpectedly as the lights kept flashing and the music blared.

"Where is Aki?" I shouted to Og, as if anyone could hear my squeaks over the noise. "WHERE'S AKI?"

Mrs. Brisbane shut the thing off.

"Show it to Humphrey," Simon suggested.

"Yes, show Humphrey," the other students begged.

So Mrs. Brisbane brought the ball over to our table and set it down in front of my cage.

"I hope Aki doesn't scare you, Humphrey, but here goes." She pressed a button on the ball and it all began again: the flashing lights, the looping and twirling and that song, "Rockin' Aki! Rock 'n' roll rules!"

Now I could see what everyone was laughing at. Aki, a tiny toy hamster with wild, rainbow-striped fur, was rolling around in the hamster ball. Somehow, as the ball turned, he always remained upright as he danced.

I wasn't scared—not one bit. But I was quite impressed!

"Rockin' Aki!" I squeaked along. Of course, no one heard me. I couldn't even hear myself. "Rock 'n' roll rules!"

I was truly sorry when Mrs. Brisbane switched Aki off.

"I think that's enough rocking and rolling for today," she said.

Some of the kids moaned and I agreed with them.

Mrs. Brisbane returned the ball to her desk. "So now you know what I did this summer. I also sent letters to all of your homes asking you to bring in a box with something that represents your summer. Who would like to share next?"

I just had to squeak up for myself. "Hey, nobody sent me a letter!"

"BOING-BOING!" Og added.

Some hands went up in the air and Mrs. Brisbane called on Simon. "Say your name first," she said.

Simon jumped up out of his chair, opened his box and took out a photo of a very familiar place.

"Simon Morgenstern. Here's where I went. Camp Happy Hollow. They had a Howler and I was a Blue Jay and I burped the loudest and . . ."

Mrs. Brisbane interrupted him. "Slow-Down-Simon," she said. "Take your time."

Simon tried to slow down and told the class about some of the adventures he'd had at Happy Hollow. I'd had adventures there, too, but of course, I didn't have a box because *no one told me to bring one.*

One by one, the other students shared their summer stories. Rosie had gone to a different camp. She held up a medal she won for winning a wheelchair race and a picture of her crossing the finish line. Boy, that Rosie could roll!

Harry held up a T-shirt that said I Survived the Blaster and told about riding a REALLY-REALLY-REALLY fast roller coaster. It sounded unsqueakably exciting to me!

Small-Paul had taken a computer class and showed us a page of something he called "code," but it looked like gibberish to me.

15

Tall-Paul had a collection of pinecones from his family's camping trip in the mountains.

Holly held up an ear of corn she had grown herself when she visited her grandparents on a farm.

"I helped Grandma and Grandpa a lot," she said. "I fed the chickens and weeded the garden, picked the vegetables and took care of the dogs."

"My, that was helpful of you, Holly," Mrs. Brisbane agreed.

"And I rode a tractor and rode a horse and collected the eggs," the girl went on.

"Thank you, Holly."

Next, Mrs. Brisbane called on a boy waving his hand impatiently.

"I'm Thomas T. True," said a boy as he opened up a big box. "And I went fishing with my grandpa and I caught a fish that was *huge*. It was bigger than I am!"

I was impressed and I guess the other students were, too, because they were all whispering.

"Quiet, students," Mrs. Brisbane told them. "Go on, Thomas."

"That fish was so big, it filled up the whole boat, so Grandpa and I had to swim to shore and pull the boat with us. Man, we ate fish for the rest of the summer!" Thomas's eyes sparkled.

"Do you have a picture of it?" Small-Paul asked.

"Nope. We were too busy wrestling the fish to take a picture. So I brought Grandpa's favorite fly instead," Thomas said, reaching in the box.

"BOING-BOING!" Og leaped with excitement when he heard the word *fly*. After all, frogs think insects like flies are yummy. But the thing Thomas took out of the box wasn't even an insect. It was a goofy, feathery-looking thing.

"Grandpa ties his own flies. The fish think they're real flies," he explained.

I hoped Og wasn't too disappointed that the flies were fake.

"About that big fish," Mrs. Brisbane said. "How did you get it in the boat if it was bigger than you?"

Thomas shook his head. "It wasn't easy, teacher. It sure wasn't easy."

Mrs. Brisbane told Thomas he could sit down and called on Kelsey.

My mind was racing with thoughts of a BIG-BIG-BIG fish that could probably eat a hamster *and* a frog if it wanted. But then I heard Kelsey say, "Broken arm."

A broken arm sounded painful, so I listened carefully to her story. "It was the last day of school. I was so happy it was vacation, when I got off the bus, I raced home. But I tripped coming up the front walk and broke my arm." She sighed. "I was in a cast most of the summer. I couldn't go swimming even once!"

She opened her box and brought out a sling and a picture of her with a broken arm.

"The summer before that, I broke my leg!" Kelsey explained.

"I'm so sorry, Kelsey," Mrs. Brisbane said.

17

I was sorry, too.

"Who's left?" Mrs. Brisbane asked. "Joseph? I mean, Joey?"

Joey stood up, but he didn't look anxious to talk. "I didn't do anything," he said. "I just stayed home."

"A stay-at-home vacation can be a lot of fun," the teacher said.

Joey shrugged. "It was okay. I played with my dog, Skipper, a lot." He reached in his box and pulled out a Frisbee. "He likes to catch this. He can leap way up and catch it in his teeth. He never misses. See? There are teeth marks all around the edge."

I was starting to like Joey, but when I heard about Skipper's leaping and his teeth, I wasn't so sure. My experience with dogs has taught me that they are not especially friendly to hamsters and other small, furry creatures.

Mrs. Brisbane glanced down at the class list. "And who else is left? Phoebe Pratt?"

The girl called Phoebe didn't stand up. She just sat there, staring down at her table.

"I forgot," she said.

"You mean you left your box at home?" Mrs. Brisbane asked.

Phoebe shook her head.

"No. I forgot to make a box." The girl looked miserable.

"Well, you can tell us what you did anyway." It was nice of Mrs. Brisbane not to be mad at Phoebe.

Slowly, the girl stood up. "I had a stay-at-home vacation, too," she said. "But I don't have a dog."

"Can you think of anything fun that you did?" Mrs. Brisbane asked.

Phoebe thought for a few seconds. "I played games with my grandmother," she said.

Mrs. Brisbane asked questions about what kind of games Phoebe liked to play, but I could tell that the girl was embarrassed that she didn't have a summer box.

So was I.

"Thanks for sharing, Phoebe. You may sit down now," Mrs. Brisbane said. "It's almost time for recess, so please put your boxes away. But before you go outside, I need to find an assistant for Rosie."

Not even one second went by before the girl named Holly waved her hand, shouting, "Me! Me! Oh, please, I'll do it!"

"Very well, Holly," Mrs. Brisbane said. "You and Rosie stay behind for a minute so I can tell you what to do."

That annoying bell rang again and the students all left the room, except Holly and Rolling-Rosie.

Mrs. Brisbane explained that Holly would make sure the path was clear for Rosie's wheelchair, help her if she couldn't reach something, see that she got outside safely in an emergency and anything else that Rosie needed her to do.

"I'll do a good job," Holly said.

"I'm sure you will." Mrs. Brisbane turned to Rolling-

Rosie. "You'll have to make sure that Holly knows when you need help."

"Don't worry about it," Rosie said with a big smile. "I don't need much help at all."

Mrs. Brisbane smiled back. "Then I think it's time for you girls to go out to the playground."

She watched as Holly swung the door wide open for Rosie's wheelchair and closed it again when they were in the hall.

Then she turned to Og and me. "We have the whole year ahead of us to get to know these students."

These strange students were *staying*? For the *rest* of the year?

Then she said, "So far, so good."

So far, I couldn't see anything good about the first day of school. I was too busy wondering what all my old friends from Room 26 were doing. And trying to figure out exactly where they were.

HUMPHREY'S RULES OF SCHOOL: If your teacher asks you to bring something to class, try not to forget. Of course, sometimes the teacher forgets to tell you what to bring, and that makes you feel BAD-BAD-BAD.

Rules·Rules·Rules

Usually I enjoy a nice morning nap. But there was so much going on that morning, I didn't have time to settle in for a doze until the strange students left for recess. But my nap didn't last long, because when the students returned, I heard Mrs. Brisbane talking and she sounded WORRIED-WORRIED-WORRIED.

"Harry didn't come back," she said. "Did anyone see him on the playground?"

"Sure," Simon said. "We shot some hoops."

"What happened to him?" she asked.

Simon shrugged. "I don't know."

Mrs. Brisbane frowned. "I may have to send someone to look for him."

"I'll find him!" said Holly, waving her hand. "Send me."

Just then, the door opened and Mrs. Wright, the physical education teacher, entered, pulling Harry along with her.

"Mrs. Brisbane, I believe Harry is your student," she said. "I found him on the playground, loitering."

Loitering? That was a new word to me. I wished I had

21

a dictionary in my cage. Then Mrs. Wright added, "When the bell rings, students should not dawdle."

Dawdle? That was a funny word, too.

"I thought his teacher solved his problem last year," Mrs. Wright said. I noticed the silver whistle around her neck and crossed my paws that she wouldn't blow it. "But I see she didn't."

"Harry, why were you late?" Mrs. Brisbane asked the boy. "Did you hear the bell?"

Harry nodded.

"Did you see the other students lining up to come inside?" she continued.

Harry nodded again. "Yes, and I was about to get in line when I noticed this cool anthill near my foot. I almost stepped on it! It was the biggest one I ever saw!"

"So you lost track of time?" Mrs. Brisbane asked.

"Yes," Harry said.

Mrs. Wright shook her head. "Dawdling."

"Very well, take your seat," Mrs. Brisbane told Harry. "Next time, get right in line."

"We do have rules, Mrs. Brisbane," Mrs. Wright said. "I hope your students obey them."

Mrs. Brisbane waited for Mrs. Wright to leave. Then she said, "Speaking of rules, I think it's time to go over the rules of this classroom."

None too soon, I thought.

There was nothing too surprising about the rules Mrs. Brisbane had printed on the board earlier that morning:

1. Follow directions as soon as they are given.
2. Raise your hand and wait to be called on before speaking.
3. Stay in your seat while the teacher is teaching.
4. Keep your hands, legs and other objects to yourself.
5. Walk inside the school and use your inside voice.
6. Treat people the way you'd like to be treated.

As I read the rules, I wondered how good I was at following them. I *try* to follow the teacher's directions. But what can I do if no one gives me directions? For example, what if no one tells me to bring a summer box to school?

Still, those rules got me to thinking.

- The rule about raising hands made me miss Raise-Your-Hand-Heidi, who sometimes forgot that rule last year, but I liked her anyway.
- I can't stay in my seat because I don't actually have a seat. But I always try to stay in my cage while the teacher is teaching.
- I try to keep my paws to myself, and I hope that dogs, cats and other large creatures will do the same.
- I also try to remember to walk inside the school. But I have to admit, sometimes I roll (in my hamster ball).
- I always use my inside voice because even when I shout, it's not very loud.

- And I treat people the way I'd like to be treated. At least I *mean* to.

Then Mrs. Brisbane talked about the consequences of breaking the rules, which made my whiskers wiggle. A warning was bad enough, and so was a time-out. But a note home—eek! I thought that would be terrible until I realized that my home actually *was* Room 26. Next came a phone call home (but I don't have a phone). And finally, a student who broke the rules again would be sent to the principal's office.

I liked Principal Morales a lot. But I didn't think I'd like to have to go to his office and tell him I'd broken a rule. He'd be unsqueakably disappointed in me.

I was imagining myself sitting in the principal's office after breaking one of the rules when I suddenly heard Mrs. Brisbane say, "There is another rule in Room Twenty-six: All students must treat Humphrey and Og with the greatest respect."

My ears perked up.

"Did you hear that, Og?" I squeaked. "She's talking about us!"

"BOING-BOING!" Og splashed around in his tank, which made the strange children laugh.

Mrs. Brisbane explained that the students would get to take turns bringing me home for the weekend, but first they'd have to learn to take care of me. And while Og stayed in the classroom on weekends, because he didn't need to be fed as often as I did, they would learn to take care of him as well.

Then the teacher gathered the new group around my cage and put on some gloves so she could show them how to clean my cage.

"Who wants to hold Humphrey?" she asked.

Not surprisingly, LOTS-LOTS-LOTS of the new students volunteered.

Mrs. Brisbane slowly and gently picked me up.

"Never poke your finger in the cage," she told the students. "Give Humphrey time to get used to you."

"Will he bite?" Phoebe asked nervously.

"No way!" I squeaked.

"Humphrey hasn't bitten anyone yet. But if someone poked a finger in his face, I wouldn't blame him," Mrs. Brisbane said.

"When I had a hamster, he bit my finger," Joey said. "But my mom said it was because he thought it was a carrot."

Mrs. Brisbane nodded. "And if you don't wash your hands before handling a hamster, he might smell the food you've eaten and think you're something to eat, too."

I don't like to disagree with the teacher, but first of all, many humans have hands that don't smell like anything I'd want to eat. And I'm smart enough to tell the difference between a carrot and a finger!

"Let's see. Why don't you take him, Kelsey?" she said.

Kelsey looked surprised.

I'm sure I did, too. Kelsey looked like a nice girl, but it did seem as if she could be more careful.

"Hold him in your hand, like this." Mrs. Brisbane transferred me to Kelsey's outstretched hand. "Make him feel very safe. Cup your other hand over his head, like a little roof. I think he likes that."

I do like that, as a matter of fact.

Kelsey was so excited to be holding me, her hand actually shook a little. I suddenly remembered about her broken arm and her broken leg and I hoped I wouldn't end up being a broken hamster.

"Don't worry, Humphrey. I'll be careful with you," she whispered.

I relaxed and so did she. The shaking stopped.

"Can I pet him?" Simon asked.

"Gently," Mrs. Brisbane told him.

He stroked my back with his fingers. It felt unsqueakably nice.

Then Mrs. Brisbane got busy cleaning my cage. She took everything out—even my water bottle—and put it all in a big bucket of soapy water. Luckily, my mirror is firmly attached to my cage and it stayed (as well as my notebook hiding behind it).

Next, she took a brush and BRUSHED-BRUSHED-BRUSHED everything clean.

After that, she took all the soft, papery bedding out of my cage.

"What's that?" Holly asked, pointing to a corner.

"That's Humphrey's bathroom area," Mrs. Brisbane replied. "Those are his droppings."

"His poo?" Thomas's eyes opened wide with surprise. Mrs. Brisbane nodded.

"Ewww—poo!" Thomas said.

Somebody giggled. Then all of the kids started chanting, "Ewww-poo! Ewww-poo!" in a very rude way.

Mrs. Brisbane shushed them. "Come on. It's perfectly natural."

"Perfectly natural!" I repeated. "Besides, where else am I supposed to go?"

"May I hold Humphrey?" Rosie asked. "I already know how to hold a guinea pig."

Mrs. Brisbane carefully moved me from Kelsey's palm to Rosie's. Her hand didn't shake one bit.

Next, the teacher scrubbed the bottom and sides of my cage until they were unsqueakably clean.

She let Helpful-Holly and Just-Joey put new bedding in my cage, while Phoebe filled my water bottle and Paul F. put fresh Nutri-Nibbles in my feeder. Yum.

Paul G. put my wheel back in and made sure it was spinning properly while Harry and Thomas put everything else back in place.

"It looks and smells a lot better now, Humphrey," Mrs. Brisbane said as she gently carried me from Rosie's hand back to the cage. "Check it out."

I hopped on that shiny clean wheel and gave it all I had.

"Look at Humphrey go!" Thomas T. True cried out. "He must be going a million miles an hour!"

"He couldn't be going a million miles an hour. He'd break the sound barrier at 768 miles, and I don't hear a sonic boom," Small-Paul said.

I was impressed. But I have to admit, I felt as if I was going a million miles an hour.

"I guess Thomas was just exaggerating a little," Mrs. Brisbane said.

"Thomas exaggerates a lot," Small-Paul said.

"Now, students, no bickering," Mrs. Brisbane told them. "Let's go back to our places."

I hopped off my wheel and settled down in that lovely fresh bedding.

Phoebe raised her hand and Mrs. Brisbane called on her. "Did you say we all get to take Humphrey home?"

"At one time or another, yes," was the answer. Phoebe's face lit up.

"If you don't get a turn right away, don't worry," the teacher continued. "You'll get him eventually, as long as your parents sign a permission form. After all, families don't always have time for a hamster on the weekend."

Phoebe's smile faded away, but I think I was the only one who noticed.

I was the one smiling when Mrs. Brisbane asked the students who'd like to take me home and every single hand went up.

Maybe these new humans weren't quite as strange as I thought.

Later, Mrs. Brisbane rearranged the seating in the classroom. First, she had everyone take their belongings to the sides of the room. Then she told each student where to sit. There were a few groans, but mostly, the kids settled down without complaint, until Mrs. Brisbane went back to teaching and made some notes on the board.

Suddenly, a hand began waving. "Teacher?"

Mrs. Brisbane looked up. "Please call me Mrs. Brisbane," she said. "What is it, Kelsey?"

"I can't see with *him* there." She pointed to Tall-Paul, who was seated directly in front of her.

I could imagine it would be hard to see with Paul G. blocking her view.

"My mistake," Mrs. Brisbane said. "I must have gotten the Pauls mixed up. Paul Green, could you switch places with Paul Fletcher?"

"Okay." Tall-Paul gathered his belongings and moved toward the side of the room.

Small-Paul picked up his notebook and backpack and moved toward the front of the room. He wouldn't block anyone's view.

Somewhere in the middle, they almost walked right into each other.

"Watch out!" I squeaked.

Everybody laughed, except the two Pauls. They carefully avoided walking into each other, and I noticed that they also avoided looking at each other.

"Now can you see, Kelsey?" Mrs. Brisbane asked.

"I can see fine," Kelsey answered.

Mrs. Brisbane continued with the lesson, but I couldn't concentrate.

I was watching the two Pauls, staring down at their desks.

～⌣～

I was GLAD-GLAD-GLAD when the school bell rang at the end of the day and only Mrs. Brisbane, Og and I were left in the room. Whew! It had been a tiring day. Like most hamsters, I sleep more during the day than at night, but with so much going on, I hadn't gotten much napping done. But there was no time to sleep now. I needed time to myself to try and figure things out.

I was deep in thought when I heard a familiar, friendly voice.

"I survived!" the voice said.

"Congratulations," Mrs. Brisbane replied.

I scampered up to a tree branch near the top of my cage as one of my favorite humans, Ms. Mac, entered the room.

Ms. Mac was beautiful. Ms. Mac was sweet. Ms. Mac was amazing. If it hadn't been for Ms. Mac, I would probably still be living at boring old Pet-O-Rama, hoping that someone would give me a real home. Ms. Mac found me there and brought me to Room 26. Then she went to Brazil for a while, and I had to learn to live with Mrs. Brisbane. I wasn't too sure about her at first, but she turned out to be a great teacher.

Now Ms. Mac was back. But where had she been all day?

She sank into a chair next to Mrs. Brisbane's desk. "I have a lot to learn," she said.

"You'll be fine," Mrs. Brisbane assured her. "But first grade isn't easy."

So *that's* where Ms. Mac was. She was teaching first grade at Longfellow School!

"It's exciting, but there's so much to teach them," Ms. Mac continued. "I wish I had Humphrey and Og to help."

She glanced over our way and waved. "Hi, guys," she said.

"Hi, Ms. Mac! You'll be great at first grade—mark my words!" I squeaked in encouragement while Og splashed loudly in his tank.

"How did your day go?" Ms. Mac asked Mrs. Brisbane.

"I think it will be a good year," Mrs. Brisbane said. "Want to grab a cup of coffee?"

"Would I!" Ms. Mac answered.

While Mrs. Brisbane gathered up her things, Ms. Mac came over to see Og and me. She leaned down close to my cage and I saw her big, happy smile and her sparkling eyes. She smelled of apples.

"Maybe I can borrow you once in a while," she whispered.

"I hope so," I whispered back. But unfortunately, I know all she heard was a very soft squeak.

⌣‿⌣

Then Og and I were alone, left to think over the strange happenings of the first day of school.

"Thomas does exaggerate," I said to my neighbor. "I think that fish story was a tall tale."

"BOING!" he answered.

"Phoebe is very forgetful, but Holly is VERY-VERY-VERY helpful," I added.

"BOING!" he agreed again.

"I wonder why Harry can't hurry up," I said after a little more thinking.

"BOING-BOING!" my friend replied.

"But I don't have time to worry about these strange students," I continued. "Because I'm busy worrying about what happened to my *real* friends from Room Twenty-six—the ones from last year."

I was silent for a few seconds, and then I squeaked what was really on my mind. "Am I ever going to see them again?"

HUMPHREY'S RULES OF SCHOOL: Treat hamsters the way you'd like to be treated, which includes telling them where their friends have gone!

Night School

~~~~~~

When the room got dark, my thoughts got darker. Not only was I curious about where my old friends had gone, but I was also unsqueakably worried about what they would do without a helpful hamster to help them with their problems. I don't mean to brag, but I had lent a helping paw to all my classmates last year, even if they didn't always know it.

"No use sitting around and worrying," I suddenly squeaked out loud. "We need to do something!"

"BOING!" Og agreed.

Just then, the room was filled with bright light.

"Never fear, 'cause Aldo's here!" a friendly voice boomed out.

"Aldo!" I shouted, happy to see Aldo Amato pull his cleaning cart into the room. Aldo is the night custodian, and he's also a wonderful friend. I'd seen him at camp over the summer, but I hadn't seen him for the last few weeks.

He came up to the table and gazed down at me.

"You're a sight for sore eyes, Humphrey," he said, reaching in his pocket. "Here, have some sunflower seeds."

Yum! I'm always happy to get my favorite treat.

Aldo found a jar of Froggy Food Sticks for Og and sprinkled some in his tank. "Here you go, Og. Enjoy them in good health!"

Og swam around, gathering the little sticks in his huge mouth. I'm sorry he doesn't get tasty sunflower seeds like I do, but he doesn't seem to mind.

"So it's back to school for all of us," he said. "Back to work at night and back to college in the daytime for me."

Aldo was going to college so he could be a teacher someday.

"I have some good courses this year," Aldo continued. "Including biology. That's where I'll learn about critters like you."

I chomped away on a sunflower seed, thinking that biology *must* be an interesting course.

"Say, I saw Richie after school. I think he's a little worried about his new teacher, Miss Becker." I stopped mid-chomp. Repeat-It-Please-Richie Rinaldi was Aldo's nephew and a former classmate in Room 26.

"Miss Becker? Where is she? How can I find Richie?" I squeaked. "Why is he worried?"

I guess Aldo didn't understand. "I'll tell him you said hello," he answered.

Suddenly, the sunflower seed didn't taste so good, because Richie was worried. Even if he wasn't in Room 26 anymore, he was still my friend.

Then Aldo got to work cleaning Room 26. He was

wonderful at his job. I thought he'd be an unsqueakably good teacher someday, but I knew that once he was teaching, Room 26 would never be quite as clean again.

Watching Aldo got my mind off my worries until he saw that red hamster ball sitting on Mrs. Brisbane's desk.

"Hey, who's this? Are they replacing you, Humphrey?" Aldo laughed, but I didn't think that was funny.

He turned the switch on and roared as the ball twirled and looped and flashed and the music blasted. "Rockin' Aki! Rock 'n' roll rules!"

As Aldo watched, he did a little dance just like Aki.

After a while, he switched Aki off.

"That's funny," he said. "But don't worry. Nothing could replace you, Humphrey."

"Thank you," I squeaked.

"Richie would like one of those," Aldo said.

I wished he hadn't reminded me of Richie. I didn't like to think about my old friend being worried.

After Aldo left and I saw his car pull out of the parking lot outside my window, I decided to investigate the school and find out where Richie and my other old friends had gone.

"Don't you think I should find out where this Miss Becker's classroom is, Og?" I asked.

"BOING-BOING!" Og is always encouraging, at least most of the time.

Of course, Longfellow School is a BIG-BIG-BIG place, so I probably couldn't cover it all in one night. But I was at least going to try.

35

I pushed on my cage door. Thanks to my lock-that-doesn't-lock, the door swung wide open. To humans, that lock always looks tightly fastened. But I know that a little gentle pressure opens the door and I'm free to come and go as I please.

I climbed out, grabbed hold of the leg of our table and slid down. After I landed, I shook myself and scampered to the door.

"I'll be back to give you a full report, Og!" I told my friend. "Wish me luck!"

"BOING-BOING!" he answered.

I crouched down and slid through the narrow space between the bottom of the door and the floor.

It was dark in the hallway except for some very faint lights, which cast ghostly shadows on the walls. I shivered a little, but nothing was going to keep me from my mission.

I took a left turn and skittered along until I reached the next doorway. I looked UP-UP-UP and saw Room 28 on the door. I wasn't sure what had happened to Room 27, but I didn't want to waste time thinking about that.

After taking a deep breath, I slid under the door into Room 28. When I stood up, I was surprised to see that Room 28 looked almost exactly like Room 26—except that everything was backward! Well, not exactly everything. The chalkboards and windows were on the same side as in Room 26, but the cloakroom, the teacher's desk and the clock were all in the wrong place.

"Eek!" I squeaked.

I scurried between the desks, but since Aldo had just cleaned, there weren't many clues around to tell me who was in the room. I stopped to glance up at the chalkboard. Luckily, the moonbeams coming through the windows hit at just the right angle and I saw Mr. Michaels written on the board.

This wasn't Miss Becker's room after all.

I didn't want to waste time in the wrong room, so I slid back under the door and continued up the dimly lit hallway to the next classroom on the left, Room 30.

Here goes nothing, I thought as I pushed under the door.

Oddly enough, Room 30 looked more like Room 26 than Room 28. The cloakroom, the teacher's desk and the clock were in the same place as in Room 26.

But there were some differences. For one thing, the tables were placed in a great big circle. Mrs. Brisbane had her tables lined up in rows.

Along one of the walls was a huge tree going all the way up to the ceiling. It was made of paper, and each of the brightly colored paper leaves had a name on it.

It was hard to read the names in the darkened room, but I saw an Emma and a Margaret, a Christopher and a Ben. I didn't know any of those names, so this was probably the wrong room.

I escaped under the door and hurried to the room across the hall—Room 29.

It was unsqueakably dark in this room because the blinds were shut tightly. I could hardly even make out the shadowy shapes of tables and chairs. When I looked up, I let out an extra-loud "SQUEAK!" because there were large round objects hanging from the ceiling, giving off an eerie glow. I felt shivery and quivery until I figured out that they were models of the planets in our solar system. Thank goodness Mrs. Brisbane taught us about them last year, so I knew what they were.

I began to look for clues to find out if my friends had moved into this room. I darted to the front of the class near the teacher's desk. When I looked UP-UP-UP, I saw a sign sitting on top of the desk. Mrs. Murch, the sign read.

Wrong room again!

I hurried back out of Room 29 toward the next room. *There* was Room 27!

I took a deep breath and slipped under the door.

It was a little brighter in this room because the blinds had been left open and moonlight streamed through the windows. But a quick glance at the board told me I was in the wrong room again.

Miss Loomis was written out in large letters.

But next to the teacher's name was a list of students, and some of them were very familiar.

Miranda, Garth, Seth, Sayeh, Art, Mandy. They'd all been in Room 26 last year. So some of the students had gone to Miss Becker's class and some of them had moved to Miss Loomis's class.

Then I remembered something.

"This is where Og came from!" I squeaked out loud.

It was true. Og had once lived in Miss Loomis's class. The day she brought him to Room 26 to stay was quite a shock to me, I can tell you that! But over time, I've gotten used to my funny green friend.

I was thinking about those early days with Og when suddenly a strange sound boomed out of the darkness.

"RUM-RUM. RUM-RUM."

It was very loud and very deep—so deep, it made my ears twitch.

"RUM-RUM. RUM-RUM."

The sound came from the corner, and I could make out the shape of a tank sitting on a table.

"RUM-RUM! RUM-RUM!" the voice bellowed.

I cautiously edged my way toward the table. Yes, it was a tank, all right, and sitting in that tank was a huge frog, way bigger than Og! Instead of a pleasant smile, like Og's, he was leering. Or was he sneering?

"Hello, George!" I squeaked. "I'm a friend of Og's. Remember him?"

"RUM-RUM! RUM-RUM!" George answered. He certainly didn't sound friendly. I recalled that Miss Loomis had gotten Og to keep George company, but George didn't like Og, so she'd brought him to Mrs. Brisbane's class.

"RUM-RUM-RUM-RUM!" George was getting louder and louder. I guess he didn't like me, either, so I ran away as fast as my small legs could carry me and slid under the door.

Whew! I could still hear George out in the hall. I was

lucky to get away from him, but I was worried about my friends who were stuck in class with him every single day. They must be miserable!

I was tempted to race back to Room 26 so I could tell Og about my discovery, but the next door was marked Room 25. It was right across the hall from my classroom, so I decided to check to see if that was Miss Becker's room.

For some reason, there was very little space between the bottom of this door and the floor, so I had to flatten myself as much as I could and push myself through. The problem was, halfway through the door I just stopped.

I was stuck!

"Eek!" I squeaked. Not that it mattered. There was no one around to hear me.

I pushed again, but I didn't budge. My head was in Room 25 and my tail was in the hallway!

My mind raced as I imagined spending the night under the door while Og worried about what had happened to me. Then I thought about morning, when someone would come to open the door. They might not even see me! I might get squashed as the door opened or stepped on by students. I might never ever see the inside of Room 26 again!

Then I remembered that at camp, the counselors always told us campers to stay calm in case of emergency.

"Stay CALM-CALM-CALM," I told myself, although it's hard to be calm when you're stuck under a door.

After a few seconds, I felt relaxed enough to look at the room in front of me. I couldn't see much except a jumble of desks and the usual chalkboard. I couldn't move my head, but I could move my eyes, so I looked all the way to the right and saw desks. Then I looked all the way to the left and saw the cloakroom. In front of the cloakroom wall was a large cart filled with books. I had to squint to read the sign on it:

PROPERTY OF ROOM 25
Mr. McCauley's Class
DO NOT REMOVE!

So this wasn't Miss Becker's room. I didn't have to explore Room 25 after all. When I tried backing out from under the door, I didn't have a bit of trouble. If I'd stayed a little calmer, I might have realized sooner that although I couldn't slide forward, I could easily back out.

"Whew!" I sighed as I stopped in the dark hallway, listening to my heart pound. When my heart slowed down, I hurried across the hall to Room 26 and slid under the door.

"Og, I'm back!" I squeaked. "I'm not stuck under the door!"

Og splashed wildly in his tank. "BOING-BOING-BOING-BOING!" he called to me.

I dashed across the floor toward the table. It's unsqueakably difficult and dangerous for me to get back up to my cage, but tonight, I wasted no time. I grabbed

41

onto the long cord that dangles down from the blinds and began swinging back and forth, pushing with all my might. The cord began to swing higher and higher until I was level with the tabletop. Then I let go of the cord and slid onto the table, zooming right past Og's tank.

Once I got my footing, I hurried into my cage and pulled the door closed behind me.

For the first time all evening, I felt safe. You have no idea how comforting it can be to have a nice cage for protection.

"Okay, Og," I said when I could breathe again. "Our friends are not in Rooms Twenty-eight, Thirty or Twenty-nine. I didn't quite make it into Room Twenty-five, but I could see that it wasn't Miss Becker's class."

"BOING!" Og seemed surprised.

"However, some of them are in Room Twenty-seven. That's Miss Loomis's class—remember her?" I asked.

"BOING-BOING-BOING-BOING!" I guess Og remembered.

"George is still there, and he's not one bit friendly!" I complained. "Garth and Miranda and a whole bunch of students from the old class are there with him!"

Og took a giant dive into the water side of his tank and madly splashed around.

The more I thought about George, the happier I was that Og moved to Room 26. When Og stopped splashing, I told him more about my adventure—even the scary part where I got stuck under the door.

"BOING-BOING-BOING!" he said when I was finished.

I sighed and relaxed. I glanced around the room and saw that red hamster ball sitting on Mrs. Brisbane's desk.

The thought of Aki singing and dancing made me laugh. I began humming—or at least my way of humming.

"Rockin' Aki! Rock 'n' roll rules!" I squeaked as I hopped onto my wheel and gave it a good spin.

Then Og joined in. "BOING-BOING!" he twanged. Then he dived into his water and did some unsqueakably wild splashing.

After a while, though, I stopped spinning and crawled into my sleeping hut to rest.

It turns out that investigating *and* rocking and rolling can make you VERY-VERY-VERY tired.

HUMPHREY'S RULES OF SCHOOL: Whenever possible, try to walk through doors instead of under them.

A Friendly Face

Autumn, oh, autumn,
It comes when summer ends.
Autumn, oh, autumn,
What happened to my friends?

I was finishing a new poem in my notebook as the first bell rang the next morning and the strange students came streaming back into Room 26.

I was a little sleepy after my night of heart-pounding adventure, so I wasn't paying too much attention until a perky voice loudly said, "Wait right there, Rosie! I'll get your backpack for you!"

It was Helpful-Holly and she was doing a very good job of being Rolling-Rosie's personal assistant.

"That's okay, Holly," Rosie answered. "I can handle it."

Rosie did handle her backpack very well, moving it from the back of her wheelchair to the floor next to her table.

"I'll push you in," Holly said.

"I can do it myself," Rosie replied.

Holly suddenly didn't look very happy. "I'm supposed to help you," she said.

Rosie gave her a friendly smile. "Thanks, Holly. If I need help, I'll let you know."

"Okay," Holly said. But she sounded REALLY-REALLY-REALLY disappointed.

I was sorry for Holly because she was only trying to help. But I was glad to see that Rosie was so good at taking care of herself.

After she took attendance, Mrs. Brisbane did something pretty surprising. (But then, she's always surprising me.)

"Class," she said. "I asked you to bring in a list of three interesting facts about yourself in your summer box, remember?"

Most of the students nodded.

I didn't nod because once again, nobody told *me* to bring in a list.

"Your answers were really interesting, so I've taken them and made a little get-to-know-you quiz," she continued. "We're going to take half an hour for you to ask each other questions and find out the answers. I've printed out sheets with the questions and places for your answers."

After she gave them more instructions, the room got pretty noisy. While the students talked and wrote, Mrs. Brisbane took snapshots of each one—although she

45

forgot to take pictures of Og and me. It was too confusing to hear what everyone said, so I tried to think of three interesting facts about me.

Hamsters are pretty fascinating, I guess, because it was hard to narrow my list down to three. Here's what I came up with:

1. I am golden. (Which is true, because I'm a Golden Hamster. Last year, I wouldn't have been the only golden student in class because Miranda Golden— or Golden-Miranda as I called her—was in the room.)
2. I have a friend named Og. He is not golden. He is green.
3. I have a lock-that-doesn't-lock. (Which is true, but I wouldn't put that on a list because it's a secret.)
4. I have a notebook hidden in my cage. (See above.)
5. I was brought to Room 26 by Ms. Mac. (Whom I love.)
6. I am afraid of loud noises such as whistles.
7. I wish humans could understand me.
8. I miss my old friends.
9. You are all making so much noise I can't hear myself think!

I was still working on my list in my head when Mrs. Brisbane announced it was time for the students to return to their seats. Then she asked questions from the sheets one by one and the students shared the answers they had written down. I wished I could write the answers in my notebook as well, but I didn't dare get it out because someone might see me and find out about it.

"Listen carefully, Og!" I squeaked to my neighbor.

Here are a few things I remember:

- Hurry-Up-Harry likes table tennis. I don't know how you play tennis with a table, but I guess Harry does.
- Rosie has three older brothers. One of them has two guinea pigs. I think I'd like to meet them someday. The guinea pigs, I mean.
- Slow-Down-Simon has a sister who was in Mrs. Brisbane's class last year. (I already knew that. Her name is Stop-Giggling-Gail and I miss her!)
- Helpful-Holly wants to be a veterinarian, and she volunteers at an animal shelter.
- Tall-Paul Green used to go to a school called Golden Pines. He also collects remote-control cars.
- Be-Careful-Kelsey likes to climb trees. (Which sounds VERY-VERY-VERY dangerous.)
- Small-Paul Fletcher builds model planes.
- Thomas T. True has a collection of shark teeth. *Great big* shark teeth.
- Phoebe lives with her grandmother.
- Just-Joey Jones likes strawberry ice cream. (Yum!)

While the students took turns reading for Mrs. Brisbane, my mind drifted to the facts I'd heard.

Golden Pines was a beautiful name for Paul G.'s old school. If they had golden trees, maybe they had Golden Hamsters like me there.

I worried about Thomas's shark teeth. I hoped he didn't have the sharks to go with them, as I've seen pictures of them and they are unsqueakably scary creatures.

I also hoped Be-Careful-Kelsey was careful when she climbed trees. She'd already broken her arm *and* her leg.

When the bell rang for recess, the students raced out of the room.

"I'll hold the door for you, Rosie!" Holly said as she raced across the room.

"Okay," Rosie answered as she rolled along next to her.

Thomas was just about through the door when Mrs. Brisbane stopped him. "Thomas, where's your jacket?"

"I don't need it, Mrs. Brisbane. It's hot outside. It's about a hundred degrees," he said.

"Thomas, please don't exaggerate. It's a little chilly and you have short sleeves. I want you to check the thermometer on the window and see what the temperature really is." She pointed him in the direction of the window. Way past our table, there was a little thermometer stuck to the window that showed the outside temperature.

"What's it say?" she asked.

"Fifty-eight," Thomas answered.

"Wear your sweatshirt," Mrs. Brisbane said. "Or Mrs. Wright will blow her whistle at you."

Mrs. Brisbane watched Thomas leave the room. She shook her head, then sat at her desk, sorting pictures of the students.

Suddenly, a voice called out, "Hey, Humphrey Dumpty!"

I'd know that LOUD-LOUD-LOUD voice anywhere. It was Lower-Your-Voice-A.J. from my old class. I liked it when he called me Humphrey Dumpty.

"Hi, Mrs. Brisbane," he said.

"Hello, A.J. You know you're supposed to be outside at recess," she told him.

"Can I at least say hi to Humphrey?" he asked.

Mrs. Brisbane smiled. "Of course. But just for a moment."

"Where have you been?" I squeaked as A.J. raced up to my cage.

"Hi, Humphrey! Hi, Og! I miss you guys," he said, leaning in close. "We don't have any classroom pets in Miss Becker's class. But we're working on her. She said she'd think about it."

"But *I'm* your classroom pet," I squeaked impatiently.

"Nice talking to you, too," A.J. answered. If only he could understand me!

"Can I take Humphrey home some weekend?" he asked Mrs. Brisbane.

"My new students are awfully anxious to have him," she answered. "But maybe if there's a free weekend, I'll call on you. Now you go outside before Mrs. Wright finds out you're inside during recess."

A.J. raced out of the classroom, and I don't blame him. I'd do anything to keep Mrs. Wright from blowing her earsplitting whistle.

～⌇～

Later that afternoon, when I should have been listening to Mrs. Brisbane talk about numbers, I thought about what A.J. had said. He and my other friends wanted a classroom pet. *Another* classroom pet. Maybe they'd rather have a guinea pig or a rabbit or a frog like Og. Or even *another hamster.*

My spirits sank down to my tiny toes.

Just before school was over for the day, as the students straightened up their desks, I heard Holly say, "Simon, your backpack is too close to Rosie's wheelchair! What if she had to get out in a hurry?"

Holly *was* extremely helpful.

Simon picked up his backpack. "Sorry, Rosie," he said.

"There's nothing to be sorry about," Rolling-Rosie told him. "It's not in my way."

"It could have been a problem if—" Helpful-Holly started.

"But it's not, Holly," Rosie interrupted. "Okay?" She glared at Holly, and I thought Holly was going to cry.

"I'm just trying to help," Helpful-Holly said, blinking.

"Thanks," Rolling-Rosie answered.

I'm not sure she meant it. And I really didn't understand what was going on.

When the final bell rang, I overheard something else that was a little strange.

"Hey, Paul G., can you touch the top of the door?" Thomas T. True asked.

Tall-Paul shrugged. "I don't know."

"Try it," Thomas said.

"Yeah, let's see how far you can reach," Simon added.

Tall-Paul paused and reached way, way up. When he got on his tiptoes, he could actually touch the top of the door frame.

"Man, you're a giant," said Thomas. "You must be one great basketball player."

"Whatever," Tall-Paul mumbled on his way out.

Just then, Small-Paul Fletcher approached the door.

"Did you see how high he could reach?" Thomas asked him.

"So what?" Small-Paul mumbled, pushing his way past Thomas.

"Move along, folks, or you'll miss your buses," Mrs. Brisbane warned the new students. "Better hurry up, Harry."

Harry was still at his table, slowly stuffing books and papers in his backpack.

"I don't take the bus," he said. "My mom picks me up."

"Ah," Mrs. Brisbane said. "Well, don't make her wait."

"It's okay. She's always late," Harry said.

After a few minutes, Harry left the room. Mrs. Brisbane let out a big sigh and walked over to our table by the window.

"I always forget that it takes a while to get to know a new class," she told Og and me. "But it's an interesting group, and I know you guys are going to be a big help."

"I'll try!" I squeaked.

After all, I'm a classroom hamster and helping the teacher is my job.

But I still missed my old friends.

HUMPHREY'S RULES OF SCHOOL: Follow the teacher's directions, even if your heart isn't always in it.

Shake, Wiggle and Spin

Mrs. Brisbane left, and the room grew dark over time. Then suddenly the door opened and the lights came on again.

"Hello, mammal! Hello, amphibian!" Aldo's voice boomed out as he rolled his cleaning cart into the room.

"Hello, yourself," I squeaked back, even though I didn't know what he was talking about. Last year he'd learned Spanish. Was he learning another language?

"Humphrey, you and I are mammals. But Og is an amphibian," he explained as he started to sweep the room. "I learned that in biology."

I loved to watch Aldo sweep. He was so graceful as he whirled the broom around the tables and under the chairs, straightening them as he went.

"See, humans and rodents like you, Humphrey, are mammals. We all have fur and ears that you can see and four limbs. We're also warm-blooded," he said.

"I knew we had a lot in common," I said. I was unsqueakably glad that Aldo and I were both mammals. Most humans are not as furry as hamsters, but Aldo was an extra-furry human, especially with his great big mustache.

"Og, you're an amphibian," he continued. "You don't have any fur or hair and you've got webbed feet. Also, we can't see your ears."

That was true. I'd been looking for Og's ears for as long as I'd known him, but I still couldn't see them.

"You're also cold-blooded, Og." Aldo got out his rag and started dusting the tables. "Which means your body temperature goes up and down, while warm-blooded creatures like Humphrey and me have the same temperature no matter what the weather."

Boy, Aldo is sure going to make a great teacher someday!

I was kind of sorry that Og and I didn't have much in common until Aldo said, "I think amphibians are just as nice as mammals. Don't you, Humphrey?"

"YES-YES-YES!" I answered.

Og let out a giant "BOING!"

A little later, Aldo stopped to eat his dinner and talk to us. He always gave us yummy treats. (Well, my treats were yummy, but Og's didn't look too tasty to me. However, he's an amphibian and I'm not.)

While he ate his sandwich, Aldo told us something very interesting.

"Richie's still having trouble getting used to his new teacher." Aldo paused to take a gulp of coffee from his thermos.

"He was kind of upset because Miss Becker moved him away from Kirk. He should probably thank her for that because when he sits near Kirk, he usually gets in trouble," Aldo said.

I knew Aldo was right. Kirk liked to tell jokes and Richie liked to laugh at them. None of the strange students told jokes. So far, anyway.

"She had to separate Gail and Heidi, too," Aldo told us.

I could understand that because they were best friends. Gail was a great giggler and Heidi always giggled when she was around her. None of the strange students giggled like Gail. Not even her brother, Simon.

"Anyway, Richie will get used to her," Aldo said. "Just like you got used to Mrs. Brisbane."

It had taken me quite a while to get used to Mrs. Brisbane, and she was just one human being.

How long would it take me to get used to a whole room full of strangers?

Aldo rose and started pushing his cart toward the door.

"I think Richie's real problem is that they don't have a classroom pet in Room Eighteen." Aldo turned off the light. "See you tomorrow night!"

I was a little disappointed when he walked right past Aki's red hamster ball on Mrs. Brisbane's desk and didn't turn it on.

When the door was closed and my eyes got used to the darkness, I had an idea.

"Did he say Room Eighteen, Og?" I asked my neighbor.

"BOING!" Og replied.

"That must be where the rest of our old friends are now. I'd sure like to see that room." I was already pushing on the lock-that-doesn't-lock. "I'll tell you all about it when I get back."

⌇⌇⌇

Soon I was out in the hallway. I knew that Room 18 wasn't to the left of Room 26, so I turned right and scurried down the hall. It had those dim lights to guide me, but a school with no children in it is unsqueakably quiet.

It was hard to see the numbers on the doors from way down low, but if I looked straight up, I could read them. Just like the night before, all the even numbers were on one side of the hallway and all the odd numbers were on the other. So I read them: 24, 23, 22, 21, 20. I ran out of hallway before I got to room 18, so I took a sharp left turn and the hallway continued. There was Room 19 and across from it: Room 18.

I was a little nervous about sliding under an unfamiliar door after I'd gotten stuck, but this time the gap between the door and floor was nice and wide. Whew!

Room 18 didn't look all that different from Room 26. There were tables and chairs, chalkboards and a teacher's desk. There was even a long table by the window, like the one where my cage and Og's tank sits. But instead of mammals and amphibians on the table, there was a neat row of boxes, each labeled with a name. I skittered across the floor to get a better look and saw the names of some of my good old friends from last year. Gail and Heidi, A.J. and Richie, Kirk and Tabitha—along with names I'd never seen before.

I stared at those boxes for a long time, remembering all the good times I'd had last year.

Then, suddenly, lights began to flash. My insides did a flip-flop. Was someone in the building? Was it Aldo—or had someone broken in? Why were they flashing the lights?

BOOM! There was a loud crash. Someone was breaking in for sure!

There was a tremendous clatter—and my insides settled down a bit as I realized that it was raining outside. The flashing lights and crashing sounds were lightning and thunder! I hurried back out into the hallway and back to Room 26. Of course, *I* wasn't afraid, but I was worried that Og might be.

"Don't worry, Og. It's just a thunderstorm. It won't hurt you," I assured my friend when I was safely back in my cage.

I told him about the boxes in Room 18 and the names on them. Maybe it made Og sad to think of his old friends so far away. He didn't make a sound, so for the rest of the night, I sat in my cage and listened to the rain.

⌒⌒

It was still raining the next morning (but the lightning and thunder had stopped, thank goodness). The students arrived in Room 26 with an assortment of umbrellas, raincoats and hats, which were put in the cloakroom. I was glad to have a nice dry cage to stay in, especially since hamsters shouldn't ever get wet.

Just-Joey rushed out of the cloakroom and hurried over to my cage.

"Hi, Humphrey," he said. "It's me, Joey."

"I know you're Joey," I squeaked.

He laughed. "You answered me!"

"Of course," I said. "I'm a very polite hamster."

I wished he could understand what I said.

"Humphrey, I had a hamster once. His name was Giggles, because he made little sounds that kind of sounded like giggles," he said.

"What happened to him?" I asked.

"I don't have him anymore." Joey suddenly looked sad. "He D-I-E-D."

I guess he thought I couldn't spell, but I knew what D-I-E-D meant.

"I wanted another hamster, but my parents got me a dog instead," he explained. "Skipper. I like Skipper— okay—I love him. But I still think about good old Giggles."

"Of course you do. He was your friend," I said. "I'm unsqueakably sorry."

"Now you're giggling, too!" Joey's face lit up. "I like that!"

Well, I hadn't meant to giggle, but I was happy if I made Joey feel better.

When Joey ran off to join his friends, I told myself

58

that whenever he was near my cage, I was going to giggle.

I climbed up my tree branch, all the way to the tippy top of my cage.

More students came in, looking damp and drippy.

"Boy, that thunder last night was so loud, it shook the house and all our pictures fell down," Thomas announced when he arrived. "Even my teeth shook."

"Thomas T. True, is that really true?" Mrs. Brisbane asked.

Thomas shrugged. "That's what it felt like, anyway."

~ ❀ ~

When Mrs. Brisbane took attendance, Harry was missing again. She shook her head when she read his name, but he finally showed up in the middle of reading.

"Did you get an excuse from the office?" Mrs. Brisbane asked. Harry reached into his pocket and pulled out a slip of paper.

"Dad drove me and we got caught in traffic," he said.

I thought that made sense on a very wet day, and Mrs. Brisbane didn't say anything. Harry went into the cloakroom to hang up his jacket. The other students kept on reading, but Harry didn't come out of the cloakroom, so Mrs. Brisbane went back to check on him.

The cloakroom isn't really a room, but it's partially walled off from the rest of the room and I can't see inside from my spot by the window.

"Harry? What are you doing?" she asked.

"Just taking off my jacket," I heard him answer.

"Well, hurry up, Harry," she said in a not-very-happy voice.

Harry came out with a grin on his face. "Mrs. Brisbane, did you know that eight of the jackets back there are blue? Way more than any other color!"

Mrs. Brisbane just said, "Take your seat, Harry. We're in the middle of class."

~•~

The rain was still beating against the windows when the bell rang for recess, so my friends had to stay inside.

Mrs. Brisbane opened the closet and pulled out a huge plastic tub.

"Here's my rainy day box," she said. "The things in here can only be used on days like this."

She started taking out smaller boxes and lining them up on the desk. "We've got board games and puzzles, art supplies and activity books. It's strictly first come, first serve—no arguments. Now, first, let's get the wiggles out a little."

Then the most amazing thing happened. Mrs. Brisbane stretched her arms way up over her head and wiggled her fingers.

"Stretch . . . and wiggle!" she said.

Most of the students stood up. Rosie managed to stretch and wiggle right in her wheelchair.

I put my paws up on the side of my cage and stretched, too. I wiggled my whiskers at the same time. None of the other students could do that!

Next, Mrs. Brisbane started rolling her head around. "Wiggle your heads."

The students did. They all looked pretty silly, but I tried it, too.

"Wiggle your shoulders," she continued. "Wiggle your arms."

I wasn't sure about my shoulders and arms, so I just wiggled everything.

"Wiggle your hips," she said. "Wiggle your knees."

I'd never seen Mrs. Brisbane act so unsqueakably silly before. The students were wiggling like crazy and they were giggling, too.

"Wiggle your toes and wiggle your nose." Mrs. Brisbane even giggled at that one.

I'm very good at wiggling my nose. I've had a lot of practice.

"And now shake." Mrs. Brisbane shook her whole body. "Shake your problems away."

The kids shook their bodies and laughed out loud.

"Okay, settle down," Mrs. Brisbane said. "Now that the wiggles are over, you may come up and pick out a rainy day activity."

The students all headed toward the desk, including Rosie.

"That's okay, Rosie," Holly said, stopping her. "I'll pick something out."

"Thanks, but I'd like to choose my own," Rosie said, rolling right past Holly.

Simon was the first one at the desk, and he grabbed a board game. "Who wants to play this with me?" he asked.

Small-Paul and Tall-Paul both came forward and said, "Me!"

"Hey, Paul comes in two sizes: giant and miniature," Simon joked.

The two Pauls didn't think it was funny. Neither did I. They both backed away.

"Never mind," Small-Paul said, and he headed back to his table and took out a book.

"Og, did you see that?" I squeaked.

Og splashed around in his tank.

Thomas decided to play the game with Tall-Paul and Simon. Rosie joined them, and Holly raced up and said she'd like to play, too.

Simon checked out the box. "Sorry, only four can play. First come, first serve."

Holly looked disappointed until Kelsey asked her to work on a puzzle with her.

Phoebe grabbed art supplies and was busy gluing things to bright pieces of paper, and Joey joined her.

By the time Hurry-Up-Harry got up to the desk, there wasn't much left in the box.

"Are you feeling all right, Harry?" Mrs. Brisbane asked him.

"I'm fine," he said.

"You know," she continued, "if you could be on time at school for a whole week, maybe you could be the first student to take Humphrey home for the weekend. Would you like that?"

Harry nodded. "Would I! Yes!"

"It's up to you to listen for the bell and return with the other students. I want you back in the room right after recess." She reached deep in the box and pulled out a smaller box. "Now why don't you see if Paul F. would like to play this game with you?"

"Okay," said Harry.

Soon all the students were busy with their activities and seemed to be having fun, which was a good thing.

But there were problems, too. I wondered if Harry could hurry up for a whole week. I could see there was a problem between Holly and Rosie, and between the two Pauls as well.

I hopped on my wheel for a spin because that's where I do my best thinking.

If there's one thing that gets a classroom hamster thinking, it's a problem happening right in his own classroom.

HUMPHREY'S RULES OF SCHOOL: It's easy to get your wiggles out, but it's harder to shake your problems away.

7

A Visitor and a Visit

The next day was bright and sunny, which I normally like. Last night, I had wished for another rainy recess so I could study the new students a little more. But the sunshine helped me think of another verse to write in my notebook:

> *Autumn, oh, autumn,*
> *When the weather turns funny.*
> *One day it's cold and rainy,*
> *Next day it's warm and sunny.*

I don't believe Mrs. Brisbane thought it was funny when Hurry-Up-Harry arrived a few minutes after the bell rang. This time he brought his mom with him. She looked very worried as Mrs. Brisbane greeted her.

"Mrs. Brisbane, I'm so sorry. After your call last night, I promised myself I'd get Harry here on time, but then I had to stop for gas," she explained. "Tomorrow, I'll get him here on time."

"Thanks, Mrs. Ito," Mrs. Brisbane answered politely. Then she turned to Harry. "Why don't you go to your seat and take out your language arts workbook?" she said.

"Og, did you hear that?" I squeaked to my neighbor when Mrs. Ito had left and the students were all working. "Mrs. Brisbane called Harry's mom last night to talk to her about his being late."

"BOING-BOING!" Og loudly replied, which made some of the kids laugh.

"That's serious," I said. "I hope he wasn't too upset."

But when I looked over at Harry, he didn't seem upset at all.

~•~

The bell rang for recess later in the morning, and the students rushed out of the room. I knew they'd be getting their wiggles out on the playground, so I decided to try some of those exercises Mrs. Brisbane had taught us the day before.

I wiggled my ears and my whiskers and I even jiggled my tail (something else humans could not do). Then I SHOOK-SHOOK-SHOOK my whole body, trying to shake my problems away.

"Rockin' Humphrey!" I squeaked.

I guess I looked a little silly, but I felt good.

I felt even better when I heard a familiar voice say, "Humphrey! What are you doing?"

I looked up and saw a wonderful sight. Golden-Miranda and Speak-Up-Sayeh, two of my best friends from last year, were standing by my cage and smiling down on me.

"I think he's dancing," Sayeh said in her beautiful, soft voice.

"We miss you so much, Humphrey," Miranda said.

"I'm SORRY-SORRY-SORRY you have George in your classroom," I squeaked. If only she could understand me!

"We miss you too, Og," Sayeh added. "George doesn't like you, but we do."

"It's not the same without you two." Miranda leaned in very close and whispered, "I love you, Humphrey."

I was a little worried that Og might feel left out, but Miranda leaned in close to his tank and said, "You too, Og."

My heart did a little somersault inside me. Golden-Miranda still loved me. And I loved her back.

"Girls, Mrs. Wright will be looking for you," Mrs. Brisbane said. "She always knows when someone's missing from the playground."

They laughed and promised to come see me again.

The rest of the day, I tried very hard to concentrate on what the teacher said. But no matter what she said, I kept hearing Miranda's voice saying, "I love you, Humphrey."

Later, Mrs. Brisbane made an announcement. "Class, I'll be taking Humphrey home this weekend. Starting next Friday, he'll start going home with a different student each weekend."

I was a little bit relieved not to be going home with any of the new students, since I still didn't know them very well. However, I'm a very curious hamster, so I couldn't help wondering what weekends at their houses would be like.

⌒⌒⌒

Mrs. Brisbane lived in a yellow house with her husband, Bert. After an accident last year, Bert was now in a wheelchair. He spent a lot of his time in his workshop making birdhouses. (He made a big extension for my cage, too—thanks!) He also worked part-time at May-crest Manor, a place where people get better after an accident or an illness. Sometimes he took me there to help.

It's pretty quiet at the Brisbanes' house, especially compared to some houses, which are filled with kids and pets. Sometimes it's a little *too* quiet and I miss Og.

I dozed a lot that weekend. I napped while Mrs. Brisbane tidied up the house. I slept while she went over students' papers. I snoozed while the Brisbanes went out Sunday morning.

I was certainly rested up when Mrs. Brisbane opened my cage on Sunday afternoon and said, "Humphrey, you must be bored to tears! I haven't paid a bit of attention to you this weekend, but that's changing now."

She scooped me up and put me into my yellow plastic hamster ball.

"How about a change of scenery?" she asked.

It sounded unsqueakably nice to me.

She carried me out to the garage, where Mr. Brisbane was hammering away at a piece of wood.

"I thought you might like some company," Mrs. Brisbane told her husband.

"Always do," he said.

Mrs. Brisbane sat in an old stuffed chair near the workbench and put my hamster ball on the ground. My hamster ball didn't have flashing lights or music, but I still liked it.

"Go take a spin, Humphrey," she said. "You need the exercise."

I started the ball rolling. Things look different from inside the ball and they sound different, too.

When the Brisbanes talked, they sounded as if they were underwater. But I could still hear what they were saying.

"Bert, may I ask you a personal question?" she said.

He chuckled. "We've been married thirty years, Sue. I think you can ask anything you want."

"Okay. What's the worst thing about being in a wheelchair?" she asked.

Bert thought for a few seconds. "I can't reach that box of candy you hid on the top shelf in the kitchen."

Mrs. Brisbane laughed. "I put it up there so I can't reach it, either."

Then Bert got more serious. "People are the worst part of being in a wheelchair."

"Why?" Mrs. Brisbane asked.

"Well, I don't like it when people treat me as if I'm different. I'm no different just because I'm sitting in a chair. I'm the same person I always was," he explained.

His wife nodded. "That's true."

"And I don't like it when people try to help me when I don't need help," Bert continued.

"But you can't blame people for wanting to help," Mrs. Brisbane said.

"I appreciate help when I need it, and I know I have to ask for help sometimes. But some people just won't leave me alone. Like Violet Rasmussen next door. If I'm outside for one minute, she runs over to see if she can help. She really gets my goat."

Mrs. Brisbane laughed quietly. "You haven't changed a bit since you've been in that chair, Bert Brisbane! You're as stubborn as ever."

"It's called independent," he said, chuckling. Bert began running a piece of sandpaper over a piece of wood. "Why do you ask?"

"Oh, there's this girl in my new class. Rosie. She's in a wheelchair," Mrs. Brisbane said. "She's very independent, too."

"That's good," Bert said.

"Yes, but she's not the problem. It's another girl." Mrs. Brisbane sighed. "Something else, Bert," she said. "You know how when you were a boy, you were really short?"

Mr. Brisbane smiled and nodded. "Yep, until one year when I went from being the shortest boy in the class to the tallest boy in the class. It happened over the summer. Quite a change."

"Which did you like better? Being short or being tall?"

69

Mr. Brisbane stopped sanding the wood. "I guess there were problems either way."

"That's what I was thinking, too," his wife said.

"Me too!" I squeaked, rolling my ball closer to her chair.

"Oh, Humphrey, I almost forgot about you." Mrs. Brisbane laughed.

"No one could ever forget Humphrey," Bert said.

"Humphrey won't be here next weekend," Mrs. Brisbane said. "He'll be going home with a student from the new class."

"Which one?" Mr. Brisbane asked.

"Yes, which one?" I squeaked.

"I'm not sure yet," Mrs. Brisbane said.

We stayed out in the garage for a while, but the Brisbanes talked about other things, things I didn't understand. As I rolled around the garage, I tried to imagine Mr. Brisbane as a little boy.

It was HARD-HARD-HARD. And when I tried to imagine Mrs. Brisbane as a little girl, that didn't work either.

Maybe hamsters just don't have good imaginations.

Humphrey's Rules of School: Everybody has problems—not just you.

The Worst Class in the World

~~~~~~

I was on edge Monday morning before the first bell rang. Hurry-Up-Harry had promised to be on time every day. If he did, I'd be going home with him for the weekend. But I wasn't sure if his mom dropping him off late would count, since that wasn't really his fault.

Joey always came to class early and visited me before the bell rang so he could hear me "giggle."

On Monday, he was watching me spin on my wheel when Phoebe came and stood next to him.

"He's just like the hamster I used to have," Joey said.

"I wish I had a hamster," Phoebe said. "My grandma says a pet would be too much work for her right now. But I asked her if I could bring Humphrey home one weekend. I thought she'd say no, but she said yes!" Phoebe looked so thrilled, I was thrilled, too.

"Slow-Down-Simon!" Mrs. Brisbane called out as Simon dashed into the room, followed by Rolling-Rosie and Helpful-Holly. One by one, the students made their way to their tables until every place was filled . . . except one.

71

The hands of the clock inched toward the time of the final bell.

"Og, do you think Harry will make it?" I squeaked.

"BOING-BOING," Og replied in a way that made me think he wasn't sure.

But just as the bell rang, Harry rushed into the room and headed straight to his chair.

"I made it, didn't I?" he asked breathlessly.

"Yes, and I'm glad," Mrs. Brisbane answered with a smile. "But maybe tomorrow you could get here a few seconds earlier."

Harry nodded and looked over at my cage. I'm no mind reader, but I was pretty sure I knew what he was thinking. Maybe, just maybe, he'd get to take me home on Friday.

Last week, I'd noticed that Mrs. Brisbane spent most of the time learning about these strange students: hearing about their lives, listening to them read, sharing ideas. But this week, she went back to the routine I remembered from last year in Room 26: teaching reading, social studies, math, and science.

While the strange students seemed quite bright, I was surprised to find out that I knew a lot more than they did about these subjects. At first, this was confusing to me, until I realized that I'd studied the exact same information last year. I felt unsqueakably smart! I was sure to get better scores on my vocabulary tests this year, which made me HAPPY-HAPPY-HAPPY!

Maybe—just maybe—this school year wouldn't be as bad as I'd first thought!

But I changed my mind when two things happened right after morning recess.

First, Mrs. Wright came in with the students and marched up to Mrs. Brisbane.

"There are several problems with your class," she announced.

"Why don't we discuss them later?" Mrs. Brisbane suggested. "Alone."

"I think immediate action is necessary," Mrs. Wright said firmly. "Justice delayed is justice denied."

Whoa. I didn't know what that meant, but it sounded serious.

"Very well. What's the problem?" our teacher asked.

"Problems," Mrs. Wright said. "First, I had to break up a fight between two of your students."

"Eek!" I squeaked. "Did you hear that, Og?"

Og splashed so hard, I was afraid he'd pop the top off his tank.

"Really?" asked Mrs. Brisbane. "Who?"

She looked around the classroom, and I scrambled up to the tippy top of my tree branch so I could look, too. I didn't see anyone bruised or bleeding, which was a good thing.

"Thomas," she said, pointing directly at Thomas T. True. "And that new boy. The tall one."

Mrs. Brisbane looked surprised. "Paul Green?"

"Yes," Mrs. Wright replied, folding her arms across her waist. "The tall boy, Paul. He had Thomas in a headlock."

Mrs. Brisbane walked closer to Thomas's desk. "Is this true, Thomas?"

"No, ma'am," Thomas answered, glancing over at Tall-Paul. "We didn't fight."

"Paul?" Mrs. Brisbane turned toward him. "Did you have a fight?"

Paul hung his head and looked completely miserable. "Not really," he mumbled.

At this point Mrs. Wright suddenly dropped her voice and whispered in Mrs. Brisbane's ear. "I saw . . ."

I couldn't hear a word she said! How can a classroom hamster help if that hamster doesn't know what's going on?

I must say, Mrs. Brisbane looked surprised at whatever Mrs. Wright said.

"I'll take care of this, Mrs. Wright. Thank you." Mrs. Brisbane was always polite.

Mrs. Wright's voice was suddenly loud again. "And then, another one of your students did something *extremely dangerous*." The way she said those words, *"extremely dangerous,"* made my nose twitch.

Mrs. Brisbane frowned. "Which student?"

"Her!" Mrs. Wright poked a long finger in the direction of Rosie Rodriguez. "She was not using her chair properly."

Suddenly, Holly leaped up from her chair. "I tried to stop her! I told her it was dangerous," she said.

Rosie glared at Holly. "It wasn't dangerous. I do it all the time," she said firmly.

"I think we can work this all out during the lunch break," Mrs. Brisbane said. She started walking toward the door. I'm pretty sure she was hoping Mrs. Wright would also walk toward the door . . . and right through it. "Thank you, Mrs. Wright."

"I think I should be in that meeting," the P.E. teacher said. She backed toward the door. "*And* Principal Morales."

"I'll let you know," Mrs. Brisbane said.

Mrs. Wright was gone. I almost cheered at the way Mrs. Brisbane took control. But I didn't feel like cheering when I looked around at the classroom and the unhappy faces of Tall-Paul, Thomas T. True, Rolling-Rosie and Helpful-Holly. The other students all looked bewildered.

I probably looked bewildered, too.

On the worst first day of school, I'd been pretty sure this wasn't going to be the best class ever.

Now, I was beginning to think it was the *worst* class ever. And I was stuck with it!

It seemed like a LONG-LONG-LONG time until lunch, and I think the other students had as much trouble concentrating on their spelling quiz as I did. Even though I'd learned the words last year, I got three answers wrong! When the bell rang for lunch, Mrs. Brisbane asked Rosie, Paul G. and Thomas to stay for a moment.

"Shouldn't I stay with Rosie?" Helpful-Holly asked.

"That won't be necessary," Mrs. Brisbane told her.

Holly looked very disappointed again.

As soon as the classroom was clear, Mrs. Brisbane asked Rosie just what dangerous thing she'd done.

"I popped a wheelie," she said, her eyes sparkling. "I learned to do it at camp. You need to learn to do it to go up and down curbs."

Mrs. Brisbane nodded. I'd never seen her husband pop a wheelie in his wheelchair, but maybe he had.

"You just move the back wheels so the front wheels go up in the air, like this." Rosie started to demonstrate.

"No need to show me," Mrs. Brisbane quickly said as she put her hand on Rosie's armrest. "I understand what it is. But it does seem a little dangerous."

"Sure, if you don't know what you're doing," Rosie explained. "I practiced and practiced this summer. The camp counselors were always there to catch us if we tipped over."

"That's good," Mrs. Brisbane said. "But there might not be anyone to catch you on the playground. Do me a favor, Rosie. Don't pop wheelies on the playground. You can do it at home if your parents say it's okay."

Rosie looked disappointed.

"Is that a deal?" Mrs. Brisbane asked.

Rosie nodded. "Deal."

"Now off to lunch," the teacher said.

When Rolling-Rosie was gone, Mrs. Brisbane turned to the boys.

"So, tell me what happened," she said.

"We were just fooling around," Thomas said. "That Mrs. Wright, she's a busybody."

I wasn't exactly sure what a busybody was. Perhaps it was a person with a whistle.

"Mrs. Wright was just doing her job," Mrs. Brisbane said. "She said Paul lifted you up off the ground and you were yelling."

"Thomas told me to!" Paul burst out. His cheeks were flaming red.

"He told you to grab him and pick him up off the ground?" Mrs. Brisbane asked.

"Yes," Paul answered.

Mrs. Brisbane pursed her lips and tapped her foot on the ground. "Why did you do that, Thomas?"

Thomas shrugged. "Just for fun, I guess."

"Fun?" Mrs. Brisbane looked surprised.

"Because he's always after me about being tall." Paul looked completely miserable. "He always wants me to do things. So he said, 'I bet you can't pick me up.' I didn't say anything, so he dared me. So I picked him up. That's it."

"Is that true, Thomas?" Mrs. Brisbane asked.

"Yes, ma'am. That's all it was," he said.

Mrs. Brisbane turned to Paul. "Do you think it's a good idea to pick people up?" she asked.

"I guess not," Paul answered.

Next, it was Thomas's turn. "Do you think it's a good idea to dare people?" she asked.

"Maybe not," Thomas said. "We were just fooling around."

"Don't fool around like that anymore," she said. "If there's any more trouble like this, I'll have to call your parents. Do you understand?"

The boys nodded. Then she made them shake hands. But she didn't send them to the principal's office—whew!

She sent Tall-Paul off to lunch but had Thomas T. True stay for a minute.

"I don't think Paul likes you to talk about how tall he is all the time," she said.

"It's pretty cool. He's practically a giant!" Thomas said.

"Please don't exaggerate, Thomas. Paul's just tall for his age. Remember the rule about treating people the way we'd like to be treated?" Mrs. Brisbane asked.

"Yes, ma'am."

"Try to be friends with Paul without talking about his height. Is that a deal?" she said.

"Deal," he said.

He and Mrs. Brisbane shook hands and she sent him off to lunch.

After he left, Mrs. Brisbane turned to Og and me. "And now, maybe *I* can have lunch, too."

But as she grabbed her lunch bag from her desk drawer, Mrs. Wright came into the room.

"Where are the boys?" she asked.

"The matter's been taken care of," Mrs. Brisbane told her.

Mrs. Wright didn't like that answer. "Have they been punished?" she asked.

"It's all taken care of," Mrs. Brisbane said. "I've got to eat now."

She took her bag and walked past Mrs. Wright and out the door.

Mrs. Wright stood alone in the room shaking her head. I was afraid she might blow her whistle, but instead she just left.

"Og, do you think Mrs. Wright is a busybody?" I asked when my neighbor and I were alone again.

"BOING!" Og replied.

Then I hopped on my wheel to keep my body busy while I thought about wheelies and dares and the strange students in the class.

Maybe this was the worst class in the world after all.

⌒⌒

Later, I worked on my poem for a while.

Autumn, oh, autumn,
When everybody's busy,
There are so many problems,
I'm feeling kind of dizzy!

HUMPHREY'S RULES OF SCHOOL: Keep your body busy, but don't be a busybody.

9

The Worst Class Doesn't Get Better

*T*ardy.

It's not a word I'd heard very often. But I've figured out what it means: late.

If you're tardy, you have to go to the office and get a piece of paper that lets you back into class.

This year, I've heard the word *tardy* more often than I did all of last year. A few of my old friends were tardy from time to time, usually when the buses got in late.

But Hurry-Up-Harry was tardy a *lot*.

He got to school on time (barely) the first two days of the week, but on Wednesday, he was so late, Mrs. Brisbane had counted him as absent. When he finally arrived, he gave his slip of paper to Mrs. Brisbane.

"Very well, Harry. Hurry up and get to your seat," she said.

"It wasn't my fault," he said. "Here's a note from my mom. She tells you there that the alarm didn't go off."

He pulled a letter out of his backpack and handed it to her. She read it quickly, thanked him and sent him to his seat.

He didn't go right away. "We used to live almost next door to the school," he said. "Then I could walk. But now she has to drive me here and it takes longer."

Mrs. Brisbane looked at Harry as if she didn't know what to say. Which is pretty unusual for Mrs. Brisbane.

"Does this mean I can't have Humphrey this weekend?" Harry asked.

"We'll talk about it later, Harry," Mrs. Brisbane said.

"It wasn't really his fault, was it, Og?" I asked my neighbor while my friends worked on math problems. I should have been working on them, too, but I was thinking more about Harry's problem than about number problems.

Og didn't answer. He just splashed lazily in the water. I wasn't sure what he thought about Hurry-Up-Harry.

~•~

That night, when Aldo came, he went right to work, sweeping the room with long, graceful strokes of the broom.

"We're still learning more about you guys in biology," he said. "Amphibians and mammals."

"What did you learn, Aldo?" I squeaked.

"Mammals are born from their mamas and amphibians hatch out of eggs," he said.

I almost fell off my tree branch. "Eek!" I squeaked.

Og came out of an *egg*? Like a *chicken*?

"Of course, after they hatch out of eggs, frogs are cute little tadpoles," Aldo continued.

I wasn't sure what a tadpole was, but it was hard to picture Og being cute.

Aldo chuckled. "Birds come out of eggs, and so do some reptiles," he said. "But of course, birds have feathers. And fish have scales and gills."

Suddenly, my tummy felt a little funny. Gills and feathers, scales and eggs. I thought we were all just *animals*.

"In the end, we're all a lot alike," Aldo said. He was finished sweeping and started straightening out the tables and chairs.

"Are we?" I asked.

My head was spinning. Og came out of an egg. He was cold-blooded and he didn't have any ears (that I could see). It seemed as if we had nothing in common.

"That's the great thing about biology," Aldo said as he pulled a chair close to our table and took out his supper. "We're all living things."

He took a great, big, deep breath. "And it's great to be alive, isn't it, Humphrey?"

"Squeak!" I answered. I couldn't argue with that.

Aldo pushed a little piece of lettuce through the bars of my cage, but I wasn't particularly hungry.

"And great to have friends of all species," Aldo added.

Suddenly, I remembered what Ms. Mac had said when she first brought me to Room 26: "You can learn a lot about yourself by taking care of another species."

I guess that meant amphibians, too.

"It's great!" I squeaked in agreement.

Tardy. Again.

That's what Harry was on Thursday. He got to school on time in the morning, but he came back from lunch after the bell had rung. He wasn't alone, though. Principal Morales brought him back.

"I found Harry staring at the trophy case," he said. "He said he didn't notice all the other kids going back to class."

"I told him he'd be late," Holly said. (She forgot to raise her hand first, which made me miss my old friend Raise-Your-Hand-Heidi Hopper.)

"Quiet, Holly," Mrs. Brisbane said. "Harry, can you explain why you didn't come back on time?"

"Did you know Longfellow School won the All-District Basketball Championship five times?" he said. "But they haven't won for six whole years."

"No, Harry, I didn't," she said. "It's very interesting, but you promised me you'd get back to class on time after recess and lunch."

"I know," said Harry, staring down at his feet.

Mr. Morales told Mrs. Brisbane he'd let her handle the problem. I thought Harry was LUCKY-LUCKY-LUCKY that he didn't have to sit in the principal's office and hear how disappointed Mr. Morales was.

I was a little disappointed in Harry. Why couldn't he learn to hurry up?

～•～

"Harry, can you tell time?" Mrs. Brisbane asked Hurry-Up-Harry when she kept him in during afternoon recess.

Harry nodded. She asked him to tell her what time it was right then and he was correct.

"Have you had your hearing tested?" Mrs. Brisbane said.

Harry nodded. "I can hear just fine."

"Then why are all the other students able to hear the bell and get back to class on time and you aren't?" she asked.

It was the same question I would have asked if I had the chance.

"Just when the bell rang, I happened to be standing next to that trophy case. I'd never noticed it before," he said. "I'll be on time tomorrow."

"It seems as if you have two problems," Mrs. Brisbane said. "One problem is that your parents have a little trouble getting you here on time."

"I know," Harry said. "They lose track of time."

Mrs. Brisbane nodded. "Yes. But *you* have a problem remembering to get in line and come back to class on time. You can't blame your parents for that."

"I guess I lose track of time, too," Harry said.

"I have an idea," Mrs. Brisbane said. "Why don't you watch the clock in the morning and remind your parents when it's time to leave? It may not be your fault that you're late, but maybe you could try to help them."

"Okay," Harry said.

"Second, when you see your friends lining up, you line up, too. No matter how interesting the trophy case is or what size anthill you see. You need to take responsibility."

I agreed with that!

"You won't have Humphrey this weekend, but if you can get back to class on time all of next week, you can take him home," she said.

"Really?" Harry smiled from ear to ear. "I can do it!"

Mrs. Brisbane let him go out to recess, but after he left, she kept on talking. I'm not sure if she was talking to me or just to herself, but I listened. (I'm pretty sure Og did, too.)

"I've had problems with dawdlers before," she said. "But never quite like Harry."

～◦～

The next day, I waited anxiously for Mrs. Brisbane to make a very important announcement. Luckily, I didn't have to wait long.

"Paul Fletcher will be taking Humphrey home for the weekend," she said. "I have the permission slip. Who is picking you up?" she asked.

"My dad," Paul said.

I was happy to be going home with Small-Paul. He seemed happy, too. In fact, he looked a little taller for the rest of the afternoon as he sat up very straight and glanced over at my cage a lot.

"It won't be long now, Humphrey," he told me after recess.

Not everybody was happy, though. Harry looked

embarrassed because he hadn't been on time all week as he'd promised.

Tall-Paul seemed especially grumpy.

I know Helpful-Holly was hoping to have me for the weekend, too.

But in the end, I thought Mrs. Brisbane made a very good choice.

⤞⤝

Small-Paul's dad wore a suit when he picked me up. He had taken off from work early to get us. I have to admit, I felt unsqueakably important, but I did remember to say good-bye to Og as Mr. Fletcher carried my cage out of the classroom.

"I'll tell you all about it Monday! Bye!" I said.

⤞⤝

At their home, Mr. Fletcher got me settled on a desk in Paul's room. "Humphrey, I've been looking forward to meeting you for a long time," he said.

"Thanks a lot!" I replied, which made Paul and his dad laugh, even though I'm pretty sure they didn't understand exactly what I'd said.

My weekend at Small-Paul's house was pretty quiet, except for his little brother, Max. Every time he saw me, Max jumped up and down, flapped his arms and squealed. I think that meant he liked me. He was only two years old and much smaller than Paul. Sometimes Paul picked his brother up and carried him around.

To Max, Small-Paul was extremely tall.

The Fletcher family did fun things like watch movies and play games and eat popcorn, like the other families I'd stayed with.

Paul, of course, did his homework, because he was a VERY-VERY-VERY good student.

On Sunday afternoon, Paul cleaned my cage while Max watched.

"Poopy!" Max said, flapping his arms up and down and squealing.

I was glad Paul didn't squeal.

Afterward, Paul settled down at his desk and worked on his model planes. They had small wings and a small cockpit that were just about my size. I wondered how it would feel to fly. But then I remembered the unsqueakably dangerous boat ride I took once and tried not to think about it anymore.

There were dozens and dozens of tiny parts to be glued together and the amazing thing was, Paul knew just where to put them.

While he worked, he talked to me. Luckily, I'm a very good listener.

"Just my bad luck, Humphrey, having another Paul in class," he said as he carefully glued a wing in place.

He sighed a very large sigh. "He *would* have to be tall."

"He can't help that," I squeaked, trying to be helpful.

"Have you noticed? He's always showing off how tall he is." Paul carefully held the wing in place while the glue dried.

I was puzzled. Paul G. had never shown off, as far as I could see.

"I don't think he's a show-off," I said.

"The big bragger," Paul muttered.

Oh, if just once a human could understand my squeaks! Especially when I'm trying to be helpful.

"The worst day of my life was when he came to our school." Paul let go of the wing and it stayed in place.

Small-Paul was extremely smart, but that didn't mean he was always right.

"Someday, I'm going to design, build and fly my own planes, Humphrey," he said, looking down at his model with pride. "Look at this. A Hornet. Mach two. I guess you don't know what it is. But someday, maybe I'll take you for a ride."

"Thanks," I squeaked. "I think."

<hr>

That night, I had one of those weird dreams. This time, I was flying in one of Paul's little wooden planes. I was zooming high into the sky when suddenly a giant hand reached out and grabbed the plane.

I looked up at the face of the person holding the plane in his hand.

It was Paul Green. Tall-Paul.

"Now you know what it feels like to be tall," he said.

Then he raised his arm and let the plane go—UP-UP-UP into the clouds. I kept going and going until, thank goodness, I woke up.

Like I said, it was a weird dream.

On Monday morning, Max gave a final squeal and I was on my way back to Room 26. Small-Paul, as usual, got to class early.

Kelsey was right behind us and she bumped Paul's arm, which jiggled and joggled my cage like crazy.

"Be-Careful-Kelsey," Paul snapped at her.

"Sorry!" she said. "Is Humphrey okay?"

"Yes," I squeaked weakly.

Kelsey seemed like a nice girl, but I wished she could pay a little more attention.

"How was your weekend with Humphrey?" Mrs. Brisbane asked when Paul placed my cage back on the table by the window.

"Great!" Small-Paul said.

"Maybe you can show Paul G. how to take care of Humphrey, now that you have experience," she suggested.

Paul looked shocked. "Do I have to?"

"Well, it would be nice," Mrs. Brisbane said. "He's new to the school, and he'd like to be included."

"I'll think about it," Small-Paul answered.

I could see by the look on his face that he'd already made up his mind.

Just then, the final bell rang. Hurry-Up-Harry raced through the door while it was still clanging. He rushed to his seat and sat down, panting but looking proud.

"I'm not tardy, am I?" he asked.

"No," Mrs. Brisbane said.

He looked pleased. But when I glanced at Small-Paul, he wasn't looking pleased at all.

"Og," I squeaked to my neighbor. "We really have our work cut out for us."

"BOING!" he agreed.

HUMPHREY'S RULES OF SCHOOL: NEVER-NEVER-NEVER be tardy and ALWAYS-ALWAYS-ALWAYS listen to the classroom pet (even if you have trouble understanding).

10

The Very Worst Day

That Monday was an unsqueakably difficult day. More difficult than any day we had last year in Room 26.

First, Thomas said that he'd seen a *wolf* while he was walking to school. But Mrs. Brisbane got him to admit it might have been a big dog.

Mrs. Brisbane reminded him not to exaggerate.

Worse yet, Phoebe had forgotten her spelling homework and burst into tears, which made me feel SAD-SAD-SAD.

Next, Mrs. Brisbane asked Paul to come up to the board for some math problems, and both Small-Paul and Tall-Paul jumped out of their seats. When they got up to the board at the same time, they glared at each other.

The other students laughed.

"Sorry, guys. I meant Paul G.," Mrs. Brisbane explained.

Tall-Paul turned red and Small-Paul scowled as he returned to his seat.

Small-Paul liked to do math problems in front of the class. Tall-Paul got the problem wrong and turned an even deeper shade of red.

As if that wasn't bad enough, Kelsey skinned her knee at recess and had to go to the nurse's office.

Then Mrs. Brisbane had an excellent idea (as she often does). She decided to put me in my ball and let me roll up and down the aisles. She probably wanted to get her students' minds off their problems.

It would be very interesting if all humans could get a hamster's-eye view of their world at least once. If they did, they would probably clean their shoes more often—there really are unsqueakably *awful* things stuck to the bottoms of many shoes. Humans should pay more attention to their socks, too. On that day, both Thomas and Kelsey had on mismatched socks.

They'd also realize how much they tap their feet and move around in general, even when they think they're sitting still. As I spin around the classroom, I'm always GLAD-GLAD-GLAD I have that ball to protect me.

Despite the dangers, I kept rolling around lazily. The students were reading to themselves and after a while didn't even seem to notice me.

As I approached Rosie's table, I decided it would be interesting to get a closer look at her wheelchair. I still hadn't figured out exactly how she would "pop a wheelie."

Rosie saw me coming closer and her eyes sparkled.

"Hi, Humphrey," she whispered.

But when I got a little closer, Holly let out a yelp and grabbed my hamster ball, picking it up so quickly I was doing somersaults inside.

"Eek!" I squeaked.

"What is it, Holly?" the teacher asked.

"Humphrey could trip up Rosie's wheelchair! He got way too close," she said, holding up the ball. "But I've got him now."

"He wasn't too close," Rosie protested. "I saw him there."

"I think it's dangerous," Holly said.

"The way you picked him up is dangerous," Rosie replied. "You could have hurt poor little Humphrey."

I don't like to think of myself as "poor little" anything, but she was right. I wasn't hurt, but I was definitely dizzy.

"You must remember to be gentle with Humphrey," Mrs. Brisbane said as she took the ball from Holly. She peered in through the yellow plastic. "Are you all right?"

I squeaked, though it was a weaker squeak than usual.

Mrs. Brisbane put me back in the cage, satisfied that I was okay.

I headed straight for my sleeping hut, which was the safest, quietest place I knew.

I crawled out a little while later when I heard Rolling-Rosie ask if she could speak to Mrs. Brisbane.

The room was empty because it was lunchtime.

"You didn't pop a wheelie again, did you, Rosie?" the teacher asked.

"No," Rosie answered. "It's about my assistant."

"Holly?" Mrs. Brisbane said. "Why don't you tell me what's on your mind."

Rosie wheeled up close to the desk and she and Mrs. Brisbane talked. Og and I were as silent as could be so we could hear every word they said.

"I don't think I need an assistant," she explained. "I can do almost everything myself. So could you tell Holly not to help me anymore?"

Mrs. Brisbane was silent for a moment. "I could," she finally said. "But do you really want me to?"

"Yes!" Rosie answered. "I know Holly wants to help, but she helps way too much. She helps me when there's no problem at all. Sometimes, she gets in the way."

"Have you told her that?" Mrs. Brisbane asked.

Rolling-Rosie nodded. "I said she didn't need to help so much. It didn't work."

Again, Mrs. Brisbane was silent for a while. "I can see you don't need much help, Rosie. But maybe Holly does," she finally said.

"Holly?" Rosie sounded REALLY-REALLY-REALLY surprised.

"She likes to help," Mrs. Brisbane explained. "I think she'd be pretty upset if I said you didn't need her anymore."

"Maybe she could help someone else," Rosie suggested.

"Let's give her one more chance, Rosie," Mrs. Brisbane said. "I'll have a word with her and see if things improve. Okay?"

Good old Mrs. Brisbane. She really knew how to handle students. "Now, we'd better eat. I'm going down to the lunchroom, too," she said.

As they headed out of the classroom, I couldn't wait to talk to Og.

"Were you listening, Og?" I asked my neighbor. "Helpful-Holly will be upset if she gets fired."

I knew that because I'd be unsqueakably upset if I got fired from my job as a classroom hamster.

"BOING-BOING-BOING!" Og agreed, splashing in his water.

I thought the day would never end, but at last the afternoon bell rang. As the students gathered up their backpacks, Mrs. Brisbane took a sheet of orange paper and approached Phoebe.

"Phoebe, I have an idea to help you remember your homework," she said. "Each day, we'll put a big, colorful reminder in your backpack so you won't miss it. What do you think?"

"Okay," Phoebe said.

"I've written your homework assignment on it. All you have to remember is to bring it back," Mrs. Brisbane continued.

Phoebe nodded. "I will," she promised.

"You can do it, Phoebe!" I squeaked. Then I hopped on my wheel and started spinning as fast as I could.

I think she was smiling when she left the room.

The day took a turn for the better after school when some of my old friends from last year came back to Room 26. There was Raise-Your-Hand-Heidi Hopper and her best friend, Stop-Giggling-Gail Morgenstern, along with Repeat-It-Please-Richie Rinaldi.

I was spinning on my wheel when they came in and I was so glad to see them, I stopped suddenly and almost tumbled off. (Please don't make sudden stops when you're spinning on a wheel.)

"HI-HI-HI!" I squeaked. I'm not sure they could hear me over the loud splashing sounds Og was making.

"Humphrey! My favorite hamster!" Heidi said as she rushed up to my cage.

Gail giggled. "Og! My favorite frog!" she said as she hurried to my friend's tank.

"And you're my favorite teacher," Richie told Mrs. Brisbane.

"Thank you, Richie," she replied. "But you have to give Miss Becker a chance. She's an excellent teacher."

"I know," Richie said. "But she doesn't have any classroom pets."

Heidi leaned in close to my cage. "I'm doing pretty well raising my hand this year, Humphrey," she told me. That was unsqueakably good news. Mrs. Brisbane and I had worked hard to help her end her bad habit.

"BOING-BOING!" Og twanged, sending Gail into peals of laughter. I don't think Gail could ever stop giggling completely. At least I hoped not.

I was so glad to see my old friends from last year, I

jumped on my wheel and started spinning fast, which made them *all* giggle.

"Go, Humphrey!" Richie said.

Then Og decided to dive into the water side of his tank and made an extra-big splash, which made them giggle even louder.

"Awesome, Og!" Heidi said.

"I think Og and Humphrey are glad to see you," Mrs. Brisbane said.

"Oh, Mrs. Brisbane, we miss them so much," Heidi said. "We came to ask you something important."

I slowed down the wheel.

"You say it, Richie," Gail said.

"Okay." Richie suddenly looked serious and he cleared his throat. "Mrs. Brisbane, we don't think it's fair that you have two classroom pets in Room Twenty-six and we don't have any in Room Eighteen. We were hoping you'd donate one of yours to Miss Becker."

Thank goodness I'd hopped off my wheel or I'd have fallen over. I was REALLY-REALLY-REALLY surprised—and so was Mrs. Brisbane.

"Goodness! I don't think my students would like that," she said. "If Miss Becker wants a classroom pet, she can get her own. But I'm not sure she wants one."

"She'd like Humphrey or Og! Everybody does," Gail said.

"And Og came here from another classroom," Heidi said.

"At least ask her. *Please,*" Richie begged.

Mrs. Brisbane was unusually quiet. I was, too, and I didn't hear a BOING or a splash from Og.

"Please." Gail looked so serious, I could hardly believe it was her speaking.

"Please," Heidi added.

At last, Mrs. Brisbane spoke. "To tell you the truth, I can't imagine giving up either one of them. Don't you think they'd miss each other?"

Heidi and Gail glanced at each other.

"They weren't always together. Humphrey was alone in the beginning," Richie said.

I had to squeak up for myself. "But it was so lonely at night. Even scary!"

I'd almost forgotten how loud the clock sounded in the empty room and how long the nights were without someone splashing nearby.

"BOING-BOING!" Og agreed. "BOING-BOING-BOING!"

That made Gail giggle, of course.

Mrs. Brisbane smiled. "I'll tell you what. I'll think about it. And I'll talk to Miss Becker about classroom pets. But I'm just not sure it's a good idea to separate Humphrey and Og and take one of them away from my class."

"Thanks, Mrs. Brisbane. We really miss them," Richie said.

They chatted with the teacher for a few more minutes, and then it was time for them to go home.

After they left, Mrs. Brisbane leaned in close to my cage and stared at me.

"To tell the truth, I can't imagine teaching without you and Og to help me," she said. "Am I just being selfish?"

"NO-NO-NO!" I squeaked at the top of my tiny lungs.

Mrs. Brisbane chuckled. "I don't think Arlene Becker wants any classroom pet—not even you," she said. "So don't worry."

"Thanks," I squeaked. "I won't."

But I did. I worried and worried and worried some more. And even though he hatched from an egg and was cold-blooded, I could tell that Og was worried, too.

HUMPHREY'S RULES OF SCHOOL: It's actually possible to be too helpful.

Brisbane's Buddies

Worried? Did I say I was worried? It was worse than that. I was WORRIED-WORRIED-WORRIED and worried some more!

"Og!" I said when we were alone in the classroom. "Do you understand what they were talking about?"

"BOING-BOING-BOING-BOING-BOING!"

Okay, so Og understood.

"I'm not sure it's a good idea," I said. "I mean, I miss our old friends." I had a funny little pang in my heart every time I thought about them. "And I'd like to see what they do during the day," I continued.

"BOING!" Og replied. So he still agreed with me.

"But what about Mrs. Brisbane? I'd miss her, too," I said. "And this Miss Becker person doesn't really seem to like animals very much. Mammals *or* amphibians. Maybe even fish."

There were fish in the tank in the library that I like a lot.

"And even if they did seem a little strange in the beginning, these new students are pretty nice. I'm making Plans for some of them. And wouldn't they be upset if one of us disappeared?" My mind was spinning like a hamster ball. "And don't forget, Mrs. Brisbane said she can't imagine teaching without us. She needs us, Og!"

"BOING!" Og said, taking an impressive (and splashy) dive into the water side of his tank.

"So, she's got to say no," I ended. "Doesn't she?"

~·~

"Richie called me and told me his goofy idea," Aldo said as he dusted the tables that night. "Imagine, moving one of you to Room Eighteen. It's a bad idea! I told him that!" The tables bounced up and down as he gave them a brisk dusting.

"I think you're right, Aldo," I squeaked. "But it would be nice to see Richie every day."

"If Miss Becker wants a classroom pet, she should get her own," he said. "There are other hamsters and frogs looking for homes."

I suddenly thought back to my early days at Pet-O-Rama . . . and of the hamsters, guinea pigs, mice, rats and chinchillas all hoping to find nice homes. (I never saw any frogs there. I guess the amphibians were in another section.)

"You're so right, Aldo!" I shouted, climbing to the top of my cage. "Tell Richie that!"

Surprisingly, Aldo stopped and chuckled. "Still, those kids just love you and Og," he said. "I guess I can't blame them for trying."

I couldn't blame them for trying, either.

~·~

101

Once Aldo had left for the night, I could hear Og gently floating in his tank—making the slightest-possible splashing sounds.

My mind was still racing. I worried about the new kids in Room 26 and all their problems. Didn't they need both Og and me to help them?

I worried about Mrs. Brisbane, who was *not* selfish. She was just telling the truth: she needed us to help her.

I worried about something else, too. Even though we were different species, even though I was warm-blooded and he was cold-blooded, even though I had fur and he didn't . . . I would miss Og if we got separated.

I crossed my toes, hoping that he'd miss me, too.

I felt restless and uneasy, so I decided to take a little stroll down to Room 18 to find out what my old friends were doing in class. Last time, I'd left in a hurry when there was the thunderstorm.

Og was unusually quiet. Just in case he was sleeping (which I'm never sure about), I opened the lock-that-doesn't-lock very gently and managed to slide down the table leg without making a sound. Then I darted across the floor, slid under the door, and made a right turn. When I got to Room 20, I made a left turn and there it was: Room 18.

Once I was inside, I got a funny feeling in my tummy. There were nice decorations on the walls and it was tidy and neat. It just didn't feel like home. I suppose if all my old friends, like Kirk and A.J., were sitting in the chairs, it would have felt more familiar.

The problem was, it was unsqueakably quiet. No splashing. No twanging. No one to talk to at night.

I wasn't even sure there was room for a cage or a tank on the table by the window.

I slid under the door and back into the hallway, making a right turn at Room 20.

As I scurried past the other classrooms, I realized that if Og and I were separated, I could still come visit him at night. I'd be able to tell him all about the problems in Miss Becker's classroom. But all I'd find out about what was going on in Room 26 would be the usual "BOING!"

As I approached Room 26, I heard a VERY-VERY-VERY loud noise.

"SCREEE-SCREEE!" It was Og's alarm call. Something must be terribly wrong!

I slid under the door so hard, I zoomed halfway across the classroom!

"SCREEE-SCREEE!"

"I'm here, Og! What's wrong?" I asked.

Og was suddenly silent and I knew what was wrong. I'd been so quiet when I left Room 26 that when Og realized I was gone, he didn't know what had happened to me.

"Sorry, Oggie, I just went down to Room Eighteen to check it out," I explained.

I reached the table and looked up at the blinds cord hanging down. Even though I am always a little nervous about getting back up to the table, I grabbed hold of the cord and started swinging, higher and higher until

103

I reached the top of the table and let go. I slid again, right up to Og's tank.

"Sorry you were worried," I told him.

"BOING!" he replied. He sounded much calmer now.

Once I was back in my cage, I wasn't really that sorry. At least now I knew that if Og and I were separated, he'd miss me as much as I'd miss him.

I carefully slid my notebook out from behind the mirror and wrote what I felt in my heart:

> *Autumn, oh, autumn,*
> *Bringing changes every day.*
> *Autumn, oh, autumn,*
> *I don't want to move away!*

For the rest of the week, I didn't have time to write poetry. I was too busy trying to keep up with all the comings and goings in Room 26. Believe me, there were a lot of them!

After several days of remembering her homework, Phoebe forgot again.

"What about that reminder in your backpack?" Mrs. Brisbane asked her.

"I forgot to look in my backpack," the girl admitted. I thought she was going to burst into tears again.

Mrs. Brisbane sighed. "I think I'm going to have to call your grandmother."

That upset Phoebe a lot. "Oh, please, don't! I don't want to worry her. I promise I'll do better!"

"See that you do." Mrs. Brisbane let her go, but that was a close call!

Then, during recess one day, Mrs. Brisbane had a talk with Helpful-Holly about letting Rosie decide when she wanted help. Holly listened and agreed to try. Still, I saw Rolling-Rosie get irritated several times when Holly wanted to push her wheelchair or tell other people to get out of the way.

Mrs. Brisbane was annoyed when Thomas raced out of the cloakroom one afternoon and announced that there was a bug as big as his hand in there.

"Eek!" I squeaked.

But the bug turned out to be a harmless little fly.

That same day after school, Ms. Mac stopped by to chat. She had problems, too.

"Humphrey, teaching first grade would be a lot easier with you around, but I can't ask Mrs. Brisbane to give you up," she told me.

I didn't think it would be polite to argue with her.

Just then A.J. and Richie came in to try to convince Mrs. Brisbane to let either Og or me move to Room 18.

"You miss us, don't you?" Richie asked me as he generously slipped a few raisins into my cage.

"I do!" I squeaked back.

"You'd rather live in Room Eighteen, wouldn't you?" A.J. said in his loud voice.

"Maybe not," I mumbled.

I wasn't sure how I felt about moving to Room 18. And I couldn't tell what Mrs. Brisbane was thinking because she was spending every spare moment playing with cards.

She'd line up the cards in pairs on her desk and mutter over them at recess.

She stayed after school and moved them around, muttering some more. I could only hear bits and pieces of what she was saying—things like, "Maybe that will help her," and, "Those two will work well together."

I am a very curious hamster, especially when it comes to what's going on in the classroom. One night, Mrs. Brisbane left the cards out on her desk and I just couldn't stop thinking about them. I wanted to check them out, but I didn't dare risk leaving my cage until after Aldo was finished for the night.

"Hi, rodent and frog. Greetings from a primate!" Aldo announced when he came in to clean.

"What's a primate?" I asked.

Aldo pulled out a cloth and starting dusting the student tables. "Primates are the group of mammals that humans belong to. Rodents are the group of mammals hamsters belong to. I guess you already know Og is a frog," he explained. "There are so many kinds of frogs, they have a whole group all to themselves!"

I was shocked to find out there were more frogs than hamsters in the world. Imagine that!

Aldo began to dust the teacher's desk.

"NO-NO-NO!" I squeaked. Mrs. Brisbane had worked so hard arranging those cards!

"Whoops," Aldo said. "Mrs. Brisbane's in the middle of something here."

He looked at the cards more closely. "Looks like she's got something planned here. Brisbane's Buddies!"

Brisbane's Buddies? I'd never heard of that before.

Aldo left the cards alone and mopped the floors. When he was finished, he stopped to eat his supper and talk to us.

"I told Maria that I'm lucky I get to clean Mrs. Brisbane's room," he said as he munched on a sandwich. Maria was Aldo's wife and a special friend of mine. "I get a lot of good ideas about teaching just from seeing what she's doing," he added.

Aldo gave me a small piece of carrot and dropped a few Froggy Food Sticks into Og's tank before he left. He was a thoughtful friend.

Once Og and I were alone again, I couldn't stop thinking about those cards.

"Brisbane's Buddies," I said. "Og, do you have any idea what that's about?"

Og splashed lazily in the water. He obviously didn't have an idea.

"Now I can finally find out for myself," I said.

I flung open the door to my cage and scurried to the edge of the table and slid down the cord hanging from the blinds.

Getting to Mrs. Brisbane's desk was easy.

Getting *on* Mrs. Brisbane's desk was VERY-VERY-

107

VERY difficult. In fact, it would have been completely impossible, except for those little bars between the chair legs. I think they're called "rungs," but don't ask me why.

However, climbing the chair that way meant reaching up as high as I could, grabbing hold and then pulling myself up, rung by rung, with all my might. (I'm strong because I get so much exercise.)

Then, balancing on the top rung, I had to reach up high again, pull myself up and slide onto the seat of the chair.

After stopping to catch my breath, I reached up one more time, pulled myself up to the arm of the chair and rested again.

Luckily, Mrs. Brisbane always pushes her chair under the desk, so from the arm of the chair, it wasn't too difficult to pull myself up onto the desktop.

Although I was eager to get to the cards, I couldn't help noticing Rockin' Aki's hamster ball.

I took a closer look. I'd really only seen Aki up close when he was moving. Now, he was completely still. He actually didn't look much like a hamster at all. His fur wasn't shiny and golden like mine, and his eyes were lifeless pieces of plastic. I felt a little sorry for him.

I decided to concentrate on the cards. One big card said Brisbane's Buddies and the rest were laid out in pairs. Each card had one student's name on it. Above each pair was a label that said something different.

"It looks like some kind of game, Og!" I squeaked to my friend. "I'll try to figure it out."

I strolled up and down the rows of cards, reading the labels: Teacher's Assistants, Door and Line Monitors, Homework Collectors.

"They're classroom jobs, Og!" I squeaked. "Mrs. Brisbane is pairing up two people for each job so they'll have to work together. Isn't that a good idea?"

"BOING-BOING!" Og twanged.

"Bulletin Board Designers . . . oh, and listen to this job: Animal Handlers," I told him.

"BOING-BOING-BOING!" Og replied, splashing loudly in his tank.

Now that I understood what Brisbane's Buddies were, I started reading the names she had paired together.

"Paul G. and Kelsey, Thomas and Phoebe, Holly and Rosie . . ." I suddenly stopped. Mrs. Brisbane had worked hard and done a good job. But I had a few ideas of my own. Since part of my job as a classroom hamster is to help the teacher, I decided it would be okay for me to lend her a paw. She needed all the help she could get.

"I'm just going to make a few teeny-weeny changes, Og," I explained to my friend as I carefully started moving the cards around.

What may seem like a little card to a human is actually a HUGE card to a small hamster, so it took a lot of time and effort to move them and line them up.

I was thinking so hard about what I was doing, I

forgot about Aki until I accidentally backed into his hamster ball. I guess I hit the switch, because lights began to flash and the ball started to loop and twirl across the desk.

"Rockin' Aki! Rock 'n' roll rules!" The ball spun wildly.

"Stop it, Aki!" I squeaked. Then I remembered he wasn't real.

The ball twirled across the cards, which slowed it down.

BUMPITY-BUMP-BUMP!

Aki had seemed like a lot of fun when it was daytime and all my friends were there. But now, his hamster ball was rocking and rolling out of control! Twice, it spun dangerously near the edge of the table. If it fell off, it would be broken forever and Mrs. Brisbane would be VERY-VERY-VERY upset.

There *had* to be some way to shut it off. I could see the little on/off button as it spun across the desk, but every time I was close to it, the ball rolled away from me.

Then I spotted some pencils lying nearby. I quickly slid one pencil on either side of the ball to keep it from rolling. It worked! The ball stayed in place, but the lights still flashed and the music blasted out, "Rockin' Aki!"

There was still a problem: I would have to switch the large button from *on* to *off*.

"Don't worry, Og! I'll turn it off!" I squeaked. Not that Og could hear me over all that noise.

I wasn't sure how to approach the ball. But if I could

explore the school, spin on my wheel and swing on a blinds cord, I could surely get to that button!

I took a running leap and jumped right on top of it. I'd once seen a TV show where cowboys rode on bucking broncos, trying their best not to get thrown off. While the ball wasn't moving, it was still shaking like mad.

"Yahoo!" I shouted, just like those cowboys.

The plastic was slippery, but I stretched my paw WAY-WAY-WAY closer to the button.

"Ride 'em, cowboy!" I yelled as the ball rocked and rolled.

"Rockin' Aki!" the music played.

I pushed the button with all my might and it slid forward. The music and lights stopped immediately. I hadn't thought about the stopping part and I slid off onto the desk.

"Ouch! I'm okay, Og! Nothing broken," I said. "At least I don't think so."

As I lay there, catching my breath, I looked over at the little hamster in the ball, staring straight ahead with glassy eyes.

"Sorry, pal," I said. "I was only trying to help."

～～

Of course, I had to spend more time straightening out the cards that Aki had messed up.

By the time I finally got back to my cage, the room was getting lighter. Before long, Mrs. Brisbane and the strange students would be back.

Of course, they'd never know about my exciting adventure. They probably thought that being a classroom hamster was easy.

But even if they didn't know what I'd accomplished, *I* was pleased that I'd done an unsqueakably good job!

I think Og was, too.

HUMPHREY'S RULES OF SCHOOL: Whatever job you're given in the classroom, always do your best. Even if it makes you unsqueakably tired!

Hickory Dickory Dock

$\mathbf{F}$riday morning, I was tired and a little jumpy because I thought Mrs. Brisbane might be upset that I mixed up her cards. I was also worried about Harry.

All week long, I'd held my breath after every bell, wondering if Hurry-Up-Harry would be tardy or not. After all, he'd made a deal with Mrs. Brisbane.

He did unsqueakably well at keeping his end of the bargain. But on Thursday, he had been late to school because his mom couldn't find her car keys. (They were under the kitchen table.)

I wasn't sure whether he'd broken his end of the deal or not, so I still didn't know where I'd be spending the weekend.

But I forgot about everything else when Mrs. Brisbane said, "Boys and girls, I'm now going to announce your new classroom jobs."

She explained Brisbane's Buddies and how the students would work in pairs. Then she described each job. Finally, she began to read off the names of the students who would share each job.

"For Homework Collectors, Rosie and Phoebe." Mrs.

Brisbane looked surprised, and I knew why. The night before, I'd moved Phoebe to the homework job.

Helpful-Holly raised her hand. "Don't you think *I* should do the job with Rosie?"

"No," Mrs. Brisbane said. "I have another job for you, Holly. Just keep listening."

Holly looked disappointed, but Mrs. Brisbane continued. "Animal Handlers will be Joey and Kelsey."

Again, Mrs. Brisbane looked surprised. I just hoped that Be-Careful-Kelsey would be better at taking care of animals than she was at taking care of herself.

Joey and Kelsey both looked thrilled.

"It really is the best job," I squeaked to Og.

"BOING-BOING!" he agreed.

"Door and Line Monitors will be . . ." Mrs. Brisbane paused. She obviously knew these weren't the names she'd chosen, but she read them anyway. "Harry and Simon."

I thought that pairing Hurry-Up-Harry with Slow-Down-Simon was a brilliant idea. At least I hoped so.

Mrs. Brisbane kept going. I thought maybe she'd ignore my next idea, but when she read the names, she actually looked pleased. "Bulletin Board Designers: Paul G. and Paul F."

The two Pauls did *not* look thrilled, but I crossed my toes and hoped my idea would work.

When she got to the very end of the list, there were just two people left.

"These jobs just have one person," she said. "Thomas,

you will be Class Reporter. That means you have to record what we do every day in a class log," she explained. "What we study, who participates and even what the temperature is. No exaggeration, okay?"

"Okay!" Thomas said as he gave her a thumbs-up.

"Holly, you will be the Teacher's Assistant. That means when I need anything done, from taking a note to the office to answering the phone or cleaning the board, I will ask you. Do you think you can handle that?"

Helpful-Holly did.

Near the end of the day, Mrs. Brisbane made another announcement: Hurry-Up-Harry would be taking me home for the weekend.

"Yes!" Harry shouted. "This is my lucky day."

I hoped it was my lucky day, too.

I was tired from all that late-night work rearranging the cards, but a classroom hamster sometimes works around the clock. And I was anxious to get to Hurry-Up-Harry's house and meet his family.

I had to wait awhile, though, because Harry's mom was unsqueakably late in picking us up from school.

Yep, I had my work cut out for me . . . again.

✦

Harry's mom was NICE-NICE-NICE. So was his little sister, Suzy. I wasn't surprised. After all, Harry was NICE-NICE-NICE. He was also often LATE-LATE-LATE. And I wanted to find out why.

I got all settled on the coffee table in the Ito family living room.

"Nice mouthie," Suzy said as she leaned in close to my cage.

"Nice *hamster*," I politely corrected her.

"Mouth!" she said, twirling in circles around my cage until I felt slightly dizzy.

"He's a hamster," Harry corrected her, thank goodness.

Suzy twirled around again, but this time she said, "Hamthter!!"

At least that was a little closer than "mouth."

Usually when I go home with a student, I am placed on a desk or table, admired and played with, and then the family has dinner.

At Harry's house, I was placed on a table, admired and played with. But dinner was a long way off.

I can't say the Ito family didn't have a clock. They had a large gold one in the living room, on the mantel above the fireplace, directly opposite from my spot on the table. I saw the time change from 6:00 to 6:30 and from 6:30 to 7:00. Each time the clock reached the half-hour point, it chimed a lovely, loud sound. Ding-ding! Ding-ding!

"Mommy, I'm hungry!" Suzy said. She stopped twirling and plopped down on the sofa.

"Sorry, honey," Harry's mom said. "I was hoping we'd all eat together, but I'll go ahead and give you some pasta."

"Pathta-pathta-pathta," Suzy said, jumping up and twirling around my cage again.

116

Harry decided to wait to eat until his dad came home, which was around 8:30.

"Sorry," Mr. Ito said, giving Harry's mom a kiss. (Which was unsqueakably nice.) "I was clearing up some paperwork and I lost track of time," he said.

The Itos lost track of time a lot. Harry's mom said it was no problem, and it was nine when she finally said the food was ready. Suzy had fallen asleep on the sofa, but the rest of the family ate together.

After dinner, Harry's mom took Suzy up to bed and Harry and his dad came into the living room.

"Wow, I didn't know it was so late," Mr. Ito said, looking up at the large, shiny gold clock over the fireplace. "It's bedtime for you, too, Harry."

"Oh, Dad, it's Friday night. Can't I stay up a little while longer?" Harry asked.

Harry's dad said it was okay, especially since he'd gotten home late and hadn't had much time with his son. They started playing a game together. I decided to entertain them with some hamster acrobatics. I leaped around on my tree branch, then hopped on my wheel and started spinning faster and faster.

"Go, Humphrey, go!" Harry said, and pretty soon he and his father forgot about their game and watched me.

"Tomorrow, we'll put him in his hamster ball," Harry told his dad.

When Harry's mom came back downstairs, I started my act all over again. I was already tired from the night before, but a hamster's job is never done.

Mrs. Ito glanced up at the clock. "Harry has a soccer game in the morning," she said with a yawn. "We'd better get to bed."

Mr. Ito looked up at the clock, too. "My watch is a little slow," he said, resetting it.

"Are you sure that clock is right?" his wife asked.

"Very sure. It may be an antique, but it keeps perfect time," Mr. Ito answered.

Mrs. Ito nodded, then adjusted her watch, too.

After Harry and his parents had gone to bed, I was happy to settle in for a nice snooze myself. Like the Itos, I checked the clock.

It was eleven.

~·~

The next morning, I sat in my cage in the living room and watched the Itos in action. There was the usual morning commotion of people getting up, eating breakfast, listening to the news.

Harry came into the living room to see me.

"Hi, Humphrey. Did you have a good sleep? Do you like my house?" he asked.

I was about to say yes when Mrs. Ito rushed into the living room, looking frantic.

"Harry, you've got to get dressed. The game is at nine!" she said. It was only fifteen minutes before nine, and Mrs. Ito was still in her robe.

"What time's the game?" Mr. Ito asked, wandering into the living room, still in his robe, too.

"Nine!" Mrs. Ito told him as she headed for the stairs. Mr. Ito was right behind her.

Harry came back down in his soccer uniform at five minutes before nine. I crossed my toes and hoped that the soccer field was close to the house.

Finally, Mr. and Mrs. Ito came back into the living room, both dressed.

"Where's Suzy?" Mr. Ito asked.

Mrs. Ito ran back up the stairs. "I'll get her dressed. Meet you in the car!"

Mr. Ito looked at the clock and shook his head. It was one minute before nine.

"Okay," he said. "But we're going to be late!"

The last Ito finally left the house at three minutes past nine. They were definitely late . . . as usual.

I was exhausted from watching the family run around like that. But I realized that this was probably what went on in the Ito house every day that Harry was late to school.

Mr. and Mrs. Ito were grown-up human beings and seemed quite smart. How could a small hamster help them change their ways? I thought about that problem all day, between naps in my cage.

Then an idea began to take shape in my brain. The Itos weren't very good at keeping track of the time, but when they did, they seemed to check that clock on the mantel. I couldn't change the Itos, but maybe I could change the clock they trusted so much.

As I stared at the clock a long time, a little rhyme rolled around in my brain.

Hickory dickory dock,

The mouse ran up the clock . . .

Suzy had called me a mouse (at least I think that's what she meant by "mouth"), and hamsters are a lot like mice. (According to Aldo, we're both rodents.) So if a mouse could go up the clock, I guess a clever hamster like me could, too, as long as I had a Plan.

I rested some more while the Itos were gone, knowing I had a busy night ahead of me.

❧

Once the family was back from the game (Harry's team won—yay!), I learned that the Itos were really fun as long as they didn't have to worry about time. Harry showed Suzy some of his soccer moves in the backyard. Then they all went out for a while and came back with lots of yummy food. Later, Mr. and Mrs. Ito cooked a big dinner and Harry and Suzy helped. And they gave *me* carrots.

After dinner, they all went downstairs to the basement and Harry brought me along.

I was glad he did, because I got to sit in my cage and watch the family play table tennis. They didn't play tennis *with* a table. They played it *on* a table, using a small bouncy ball and paddles.

Suzy was too young to play, but they gave her a paddle and let her try. Harry and his parents were very good at hitting the ball back and forth across a table with a

120

little net going down the center. The game was quite exciting and my neck got tired from turning my head back and forth to follow the ball in its travels.

"Hey, maybe Humphrey would like to play," Harry said.

I shivered and quivered a little bit, worried that the Itos were going to bat me back and forth with paddles. But Harry had a better idea. First, he put blankets all around the edges of the table so I wouldn't roll off. Then he placed me inside my hamster ball and set it on the table.

"Go for it, Humphrey," he said.

The Itos all leaned in and watched as I rolled my ball across the table toward the net. I was able to pick up quite a bit of speed. As I hit the net, I bounced off, just like the little white ball.

"Score one for Humphrey!" said Harry. "Let's give him a point every time he bounces off the net."

I don't mean to brag, but I scored *ten points* before Harry's mom said she was tired and needed to go to bed.

She was tired—what about me? But I still had lots of work to do.

Once I was alone in the living room and the house was completely quiet, I opened the lock-that-doesn't-lock and slid down the leg of the coffee table. The moon shone through the big double doors and I could see that there was a set of metal shelves next to the fireplace. The shelves were spaced close together, which was a lucky break for me, because I could easily climb up and hop onto the mantel.

I haven't had any experience with clocks, but I hoped that I could figure out how this one worked. It was an old-fashioned clock with numbers and hands—not the kind with lighted numbers. The time was exactly 11:25.

There was no way to set the time on the front of the clock, so I moved around to the back. There was a knob there, which I figured must be for setting the time.

I reached up and tried to turn the knob to the right. The thing didn't budge. My Plan wasn't going to work! I sat back down on the mantel and rested.

"Wait a minute, Humphrey," I squeaked softly to myself. "You turned off Rockin' Aki. Surely you can turn this little knob!"

I felt very determined as I leaped up and grabbed onto the top of the knob with all my might. I don't weigh much, but I hoped that if I could hang on long enough, I'd be heavy enough to move the knob.

I shimmied my body over to the right and tried to yank the knob down.

"Oof!" The knob budged a little bit.

Ding-ding! Ding-ding! Suddenly the chimes rang out. I dropped back to the mantel.

Ding-ding! Ding-ding! The chimes were so loud, it felt as if they were ringing in my brain. It was enough to give me a huge hamster headache.

Still, I had a Plan and nothing was going to stop me. The ringing stopped, so I leaped up again, hung on for dear life and the knob moved a little more. I let go, then scurried around to the front, checked the time and then returned to the back to move the knob again and again.

My paws were aching. When I went around to check the front of the clock again, I saw that I had set the clock ahead five minutes.

I was afraid to set it too far ahead—then the Itos might catch on. But maybe five minutes would make a difference.

Feeling unsqueakably pleased with myself, I looked for a way back to my cage. The thought of climbing down the wire shelves made my stomach a little queasy. But on the other side, there was a window with curtains and a long cord hanging down. Perfect! I grabbed onto the cord and began to slide.

"Eeek!" I hadn't realized that this cord would be so slippery. I slid WAY-WAY-WAY faster than when I slide down the cord to the blinds in Room 26! The room was a blur as I zoomed down to the floor, which I hit a little harder than I would have liked.

Once I recovered, I looked up at the clock. It was 11:45 by then. Of course, I knew that it was really only 11:40. I'm so glad I know how to tell time!

I had another lucky break when I got back to the coffee table. There was a footstool next to it and I climbed up easily and hopped back on the table and into my cage.

I was never so happy to crawl into my sleeping hut as I was that night.

And to think, at that moment, Og was alone in Room 26, just swimming around in his tank!

～·～

The next morning I was a little sore but anxious to see if all my hard work would pay off. It was a little later in the morning when again, there was a lot of running back and forth through the living room around 9:45.

"We'll be late to church!" Mrs. Ito said, walking into the room in her robe.

"I'm all set," Mr. Ito answered. He strolled in, completely dressed for the day.

"You make sure the kids are ready," his wife said. "I'll get dressed."

Mr. Ito disappeared, and I could hear footsteps upstairs as the whole family hurried around.

They finally reappeared in the living room again, dressed for church.

"Oh, no. We're going to be late again," Mrs. Ito said, looking at the clock.

"Only five minutes late," her husband said. "Let's go."

When they left, I looked up at the clock. It said it was five minutes to ten. But I knew it was really ten minutes to ten. The Itos would probably make it to church on time. Barely.

～·～

The rest of the day was QUIET-QUIET-QUIET. I was dozing when Harry came and picked up my cage.

"Come on, Humphrey," he said. "You can help me with my homework."

124

"Eeek!" I squeaked. I wasn't upset about the homework. I was upset because I didn't want to end up in Harry's room for the night. I already had a Plan to give the Itos a little more help.

Thank goodness, when Harry was finished, he carried my cage back downstairs to the table in the living room. My Plan was safe!

When the house was quiet that night after the clock chimed 11:00, I opened the door to my cage, took a deep breath and once again headed up the wire shelves to the mantel. With great effort, I turned the clock forward another five minutes. That would give the Itos an extra ten minutes in the morning.

Hopefully, the next morning I wouldn't be tardy. And neither would Harry.

HUMPHREY'S RULES OF SCHOOL: Homework can be extremely tiring, especially if you're a classroom pet!

Brisbane Versus Becker

G ood news! The Itos never suspected what I'd done. In fact, Mrs. Ito noticed that the clock was ten minutes ahead of her watch, so she changed her watch! Mr. Ito did the same thing.

Believe it or not, we got to school five minutes ahead of the bell.

Harry was surprised, his mother was surprised, and Mrs. Brisbane was surprised.

I was not.

"Harry, it's great to see you here on time," Mrs. Brisbane said.

Mrs. Ito looked a little embarrassed.

"Mrs. Brisbane, I know we got off to a bad start this year," Mrs. Ito told the teacher. "But I'm really going to do my best to get Harry here on time every single day."

That made Mrs. Brisbane happy. I was happy, too. I just hope nobody *ever* changes the clock again—except for me!

I couldn't wait until recess to tell Og about my adventures. But first, something even more important was going on. The students started their new jobs as Brisbane's Buddies.

"Here's hoping my Plan works," I told Og.

Rolling-Rosie and Forgetful-Phoebe went to work right away collecting the homework assignments. The two girls put their homework in first. Yes, Phoebe had actually remembered this time! As I was hoping, she'd probably figured it would look BAD-BAD-BAD for a Homework Collector to forget her own assignments.

Thomas never went anywhere without his class log, which he wrote in a *lot*.

Mrs. Brisbane kept Helpful-Holly hopping. Holly took attendance and carried the report to the office. Later, Mrs. Brisbane asked Holly to tidy up the little library in the back of the room and water her plants.

I think Holly finally got to be as helpful as she wanted.

Hurry-Up-Harry and Slow-Down-Simon made excellent Door and Line Monitors. When it was time for recess, Simon opened the door and Harry led the students down the hall (he couldn't dawdle if he was first in line!). Then Simon closed the door and made sure there were no stragglers at the end of the line (so there was no way for him to race ahead!).

∿

After lunch, there was free time for Tall-Paul and Small-Paul to work on the bulletin board. This was the pair I was most interested in, since they'd never actually talked to each other before.

127

It was a little hard for me to see what they were doing. I was in my hamster ball while Mrs. Brisbane watched Just-Joey clean up my cage. Once she got him started, she moved over to Og's tank to teach Be-Careful-Kelsey how to take care of *him*.

"I hope she's careful with you, Og!" I squeaked, knowing that Joey wouldn't be able to understand me.

"BOING-BOING!" Og twanged cheerfully.

While Joey was working, he talked to me.

"I can't believe it, Humphrey. I got the best job of all! Good things hardly ever happen to me," he said.

I'd never seen Joey so happy. As he put me back in my cage, he said, "It's just like having Giggles back. I can hardly wait until you come home with me."

"Me either," I squeaked, before I remembered Joey had that Frisbee-catching dog.

Then I climbed up to the top of my cage to get a better look at the two Pauls. They were taking down papers and old thumbtacks that were still on the bulletin board. Tall-Paul handled the top part of the board while Small-Paul handled the bottom part. They weren't talking to each other, but at least they were working together.

Near the end of the day, Mrs. Brisbane called Holly up to her desk and told her that she was doing a wonderful job.

"I was thinking, Holly. Being my assistant takes up a lot of time. Maybe it would make sense for Phoebe to be Rosie's assistant," she suggested. "After all, they are Homework Collectors together."

Helpful-Holly looked relieved. "I think that's a good idea," she said. "If it's okay with Rosie."

"I'll ask her," Mrs. Brisbane said.

Of course, when she asked Rosie, it was no problem. And when she asked Phoebe to be Rosie's new assistant, Phoebe's face lit up.

Yes, my evening rearranging the Brisbane's Buddies cards was definitely paying off. And the worst class ever was looking a lot better. I was pretty pleased with myself for a while.

But after school, something happened that shook me down to the very tips of my paws.

Miss Becker paid a visit to Room 26!

<hr>

I'd never actually seen Miss Becker before. She was a short woman with great big glasses that made her eyes look huge. That might have been a little weird, but Miss Becker also had a great big smile that made me like her.

"I hope you don't mind, Sue," she said as she came in the room. "My students are very anxious for us to get a classroom pet, but I've never had one before."

Mrs. Brisbane smiled. "My class was very fond of Humphrey and Og last year."

"Oh, I know! That's all I hear. Humphrey this and Og that. That's just about all they talk about," Miss Becker explained. "But I don't know. I never even had a pet as a child."

"Why don't you come over and meet them?" Mrs. Brisbane suggested.

My heart sank down to the bottom of my toes. Was Mrs. Brisbane really going to give one—or both—of us away?

"I wasn't interested in having a hamster last year, either," Mrs. Brisbane said. I remembered that well.

"Then Ms. Mac brought Humphrey in while I was gone," she continued. "He added a lot to the classroom. So when Angie Loomis needed to get Og out of her classroom, I was happy to take him. It's funny, because sometimes I think they've actually become friends."

Sometimes? Og and I are friends *all* the time.

"But do you have to, you know, *touch* them?" Miss Becker said. Her big smile had disappeared.

"Sure, I do, but I don't mind," she said.

Miss Becker leaned in close to my cage, so close her eyes seemed gigantic.

"They say Humphrey does many cute things," she said, her voice quivering a little.

Mrs. Brisbane chuckled. "I should say so! Show her, Humphrey."

I've never been shy about showing off my great gymnastic abilities. After all, it seems to please humans to watch me leaping, spinning, rolling and climbing and to hear me say SQUEAK-SQUEAK-SQUEAK! But I was a little nervous about showing off so much that Miss Becker would want to move me to Room 18. Especially since she didn't even want to touch me.

But I always try to do what Mrs. Brisbane asks, so with a heavy heart, I hopped on my wheel and began to spin.

"Oh my!" Miss Becker's big eyes grew even wider. "He's certainly active."

She didn't sound too pleased about that, so I decided to be a little more active. I jumped off the wheel and climbed up my tree branch as fast as my little legs could carry me. When I got to the top, I leaped onto the side of the cage.

Miss Becker gasped. "How does he do that?"

"He's a very clever guy," Mrs. Brisbane said proudly. "But Og is no slouch either," she said.

I had a chance to catch my breath while the two teachers turned their attention to Og's tank.

"He's a very handsome frog, isn't he?" Mrs. Brisbane asked.

Now, I consider Og a very fine fellow, but handsome? With that green skin, no fur at all, the huge mouth and those big googly eyes . . . which suddenly reminded me a lot of Miss Becker's eyes.

"BOING!" Og twanged. It was a pleasant sort of reply, but Miss Becker jumped back from the tank.

"What was that?" she asked.

"That's the kind of sound he makes." Mrs. Brisbane was being very patient.

"And what does he do?" Miss Becker asked.

"He spends part of his time on the dry part of his tank and part of his time in the water," Mrs. Brisbane explained.

Og must have been listening (with those ears I can't see), because he suddenly leaped into the water and began splashing wildly.

131

"Oh, my," Miss Becker exclaimed. "He's awfully noisy, isn't he?"

I'd had it then. We'd been very polite to Miss Becker, but she certainly wasn't polite to us.

"Not as noisy as *you* are!" I squeaked.

Miss Becker looked back and forth between Og and me.

"How do you manage it all?" she asked.

"Oh, the children do most of the work," Mrs. Brisbane said. "Though I do enjoy bringing them home when I can. I think the point is something Ms. Mac told me when she brought Humphrey to Room Twenty-six. You can learn a lot about yourself by taking care of another species. That's proved to be very true."

Miss Becker stared at Og and me for a while before she spoke again. "I don't know what to say. The students love them so much."

Just then, Ms. Mac came in. "Am I interrupting something?" she asked.

"No! You're the perfect person to talk to," Mrs. Brisbane said.

She was right. Ms. Mac was a perfect person . . . at least to me.

"Some of my old students are begging for a classroom pet and Arlene's trying to decide whether to get one," Mrs. Brisbane explained. "So she came to look at Humphrey and Og."

Ms. Mac smiled her wonderful, warm smile. "Any class would do better with those two."

For once, I was sorry Ms. Mac had come to visit. I didn't want her to talk Miss Becker into taking me away.

"Thanks for your time, Sue," Miss Becker said. "I still have a lot to think about."

After Miss Becker left, Ms. Mac wanted to talk to Mrs. Brisbane.

"It's great to see my students learning to read," she said. "But some of them are having a hard time, and I want them to see how much fun books can be."

Mrs. Brisbane nodded. "That gives me an idea. We could work together."

She glanced at the clock. "I've got to go now. I'll give you a call tonight and we'll talk."

Just before Ms. Mac left, she bent down so she was eye level with my cage and Og's tank.

"Maybe my students need a classroom pet, too," she said.

Suddenly, I had a sinking feeling that *both* Og and I would be leaving Room 26!

～∽～

When Aldo came in to clean that night, it was clear right away that he was still upset.

"Richie called and said he thinks one of you is coming to Miss Becker's class," he said. "I don't think that's a good idea!"

"Me either!" I squeaked loudly.

"BOING-BOING-BOING!" Og agreed.

"Of course, those kids love you," he said, calming

down as he swept the floor. "But the new kids need you, too."

It was true. Just about everybody seemed to need a helpful hamster.

~•~

Later that night, after Aldo left and Og was quiet, I slipped my little notebook out from its hiding place and started a couple of lists.

Reasons to stay in Room 26:
- *Mrs. Brisbane relies on me*
- *The new students have a lot of problems and need help*
- *To stay with Og (I hope)*

Reasons for me to move to Room 18:
- *To be with my old friends: Richie, Heidi, Gail, Kirk, Tabitha, A.J.*
- *To teach Miss Becker about pets*

Reasons for Og to move to Room 18:
- *To be with his old friends: Richie, Heidi, Gail, Kirk, Tabitha, A.J.*
- *To teach Miss Becker about pets*

I stared at those lists for hours and hours and hours, but I couldn't decide which would be the best choice for me.

In the end, I wouldn't make the decision, anyway. But just before I tucked my notebook away for the night, I worked on my poem.

> *Autumn, oh, autumn,*
> *The golden leaves are blowing.*
> *Autumn, oh, autumn,*
> *I don't know where I'm going!*

HUMPHREY'S RULES OF SCHOOL: Make sure you do your part to make your classroom a better place.

Working Together

The next day, I was pleased to see that Phoebe remembered her homework again! I was certainly glad I'd changed the cards to make her a Homework Collector.

Holly seemed really happy being helpful all day long, especially because Mrs. Brisbane kept her BUSY-BUSY-BUSY.

Slow-Down-Simon had slowed down quite a bit because as Door and Line Monitor, he had to wait for the rest of the students to line up. Hurry-Up-Harry was never tardy after recess or lunch because he *had* to leave when the other students did. (And he was never late in the morning, either. I guess the Itos still hadn't figured out the living room clock was fast.)

Be-Careful-Kelsey was extremely careful when she handed Og out of his tank.

"Don't be scared, Og," she said. "I'd never let anything happen to a special frog like you."

Just-Joey tidied up my cage again, even though it didn't really need it. When Mrs. Brisbane came to check on him, she told him he'd done such a good job, she'd let him train all future Animal Handlers.

Joey was overjoyed. "Did you hear that, Humphrey?" he asked me later. "I'm a Trainer now, not just a Handler. Mrs. Brisbane really trusts me."

I could see Joey's job was doing him a lot of good. In fact, all of Brisbane's Buddies seemed happy with their jobs . . . except two of them.

Tall-Paul and Small-Paul had worked together to clear the bulletin board, but they still hadn't put anything up there. Mrs. Brisbane had taken out boxes full of art supplies and paper, maps and posters, but they just couldn't seem to agree on what to put up. Small-Paul wanted to make the theme about autumn. Tall-Paul wanted to make the theme about animals. Then Small-Paul wanted the bulletin board to be about airplanes and Tall-Paul wanted it to be about cars.

"How about airplanes *and* cars? Transportation," Mrs. Brisbane suggested.

The Pauls didn't think those went together.

I thought that the two *Pauls* didn't go together. I had obviously made an unsqueakably bad mistake when I decided to pair them up.

"Mrs. Brisbane, I don't think Paul G. and I make very good Brisbane's Buddies," Small-Paul told Mrs. Brisbane after lunch on Tuesday. "Maybe you should switch us with somebody else."

"You have to learn to work with people who aren't like you," the teacher explained. "You'll have to do it many times in your life."

Small-Paul looked miserable. "He won't even try."

137

"And what about you? Are you trying?" Mrs. Brisbane asked.

Small-Paul didn't answer.

"You can do it, Paul!" I squeaked from my cage.

Og tried to be encouraging, too. "BOING-BOING!" he twanged.

Mrs. Brisbane looked over at us. "Look at those two. Can you think of two animals who are less alike than Og and Humphrey?"

"That's right! He's an amphibian and I'm a mammal!" I agreed.

"And yet, they share that table and actually seem to enjoy each other's company," Mrs. Brisbane continued.

"He's cold-blooded and I'm warm-blooded!" I added.

"So I think two boys who are the same age and in the same class and both like things like planes and cars can learn to work together, don't you?" Mrs. Brisbane certainly made sense to me.

"I guess," Paul said. He didn't sound convinced, though.

"So give it another try," Mrs. Brisbane told him. "For Humphrey and Og, okay?"

I crossed my toes and hoped they'd try.

They did have a chance to work together later in the day, but they didn't talk at all. They just stared down at the boxes of art supplies.

Something I hadn't planned for happened next. Mrs. Brisbane asked Holly to return some playground equipment to Mrs. Wright. There were several bats and a box of balls.

Helpful-Holly had a little trouble carrying them all at one time. The bats crashed to the ground, the box tipped over and the balls bounced all over the floor. She picked them up, then admitted she needed some help.

"Would you like to ask someone else to help?" Mrs. Brisbane asked.

Holly looked around the room, and I almost fell off my tree branch when she picked Rolling-Rosie. The smile on Rosie's face told me she was pleasantly surprised.

"I can carry the box on my lap," Rosie suggested. "You can take the bats."

"Good idea," said Holly.

After they had left, Mrs. Brisbane told the rest of the class, "That's what I like to see in my classroom. Working together. That's why I came up with Brisbane's Buddies."

Small-Paul glanced at Tall-Paul when he heard those words.

I couldn't hear him, but he said something to Tall-Paul, who nodded. Soon, they were actually talking as they pulled things out of the box.

A little later, Small-Paul asked, "Mrs. Brisbane, could we borrow your pictures of the kids in the class and go to the library? We need to scan them into the computer."

She was surprised, but of course she said yes and wrote a note to Mr. Fitch, the librarian.

The Pauls were both smiling when they came back.

After school, Mrs. Brisbane seemed unsqueakably pleased with herself. Just before she left, she came over to our table to say good-bye.

"Brisbane's Buddies seems to be working out," she said. "Even though I'm still not sure how those cards got switched around. Did Aldo do it?" She laughed. "You wouldn't tell on him if he did."

Which was true.

～•～

The next morning, Small-Paul and Tall-Paul—together—asked Mrs. Brisbane if they could put up their bulletin board during recess.

"Yes," she said. "I just hope Mrs. Wright doesn't find out. She wants all students to get fresh air."

Tall-Paul laughed, ran over to the window, opened it and took a deep breath. "There. I've gotten my fresh air."

Small-Paul raced over and did the same thing. "Me too," he said.

Then they returned to the bulletin board.

"I made a plan," Small-Paul said, showing Tall-Paul a piece of paper. I was glad to hear someone else in Room 26 made plans besides just me.

Tall-Paul studied it carefully. "That should work," he said. "I guess I'll take the top part."

"Okay," Small-Paul replied. "I'll take the bottom."

I climbed up to the tippy top of my cage to watch as the bulletin board magically came to life.

Tall-Paul put up letters across the top reading BRISBANE'S BUDDIES—WE WORK TOGETHER.

Meanwhile, on the lower half of the board, Small-Paul put up pictures of students Mrs. Brisbane had taken on the first day of school. The boys had enlarged them on the computer and printed them out. He put them in pairs according to their jobs.

Next, Tall-Paul put pictures on the upper half of the board.

When they got to the middle, they worked together and didn't seem to mind one bit.

They worked quickly in order to finish before recess ended.

"Now add the drawings we did last night," Tall-Paul said.

Soon, the job titles were accompanied by drawings the boys had made depicting each job. For Animal Handlers, there were excellent drawings of Og and me.

Suddenly, I had an awful thought. "They won't need two Animal Handlers if they move one of us to Room Eighteen," I told Og.

Og splashed loudly in his tank. They were angry kinds of splashes.

By the time the other students in the room returned, the bulletin board was finished and it looked GREAT-GREAT-GREAT.

All the kids seemed to enjoy having their pictures on the board. I enjoyed having mine up there, too. But what I really enjoyed was seeing that my Plan worked after all!

Small-Paul and Tall-Paul walked out of the classroom together at the end of the day, talking about getting together with their planes and cars. I don't think either of them noticed that they weren't the same size.

∿

"Whew!" I said when Og and I were alone again. "We did it, but it was a lot of work."

"BOING-BOING-BOING!" Og agreed.

Aldo came in later to clean the room. "I'm glad to see you two are still together," he said. "Richie told me that Miss Becker said she'd decided on which classroom pet she wanted."

My tummy did a flip-flop. "Which one of us is it?" I squeaked.

"She said it would be a surprise," Aldo added as he swept under our table. "She'll tell them tomorrow. Oh, and she said Ms. Mac helped her make up her mind."

My tummy did a somersault. Ms. Mac LOVED-LOVED-LOVED me, so of course, she told Miss Becker to pick me. I still missed my old friends from last year. So why did I feel sad about leaving Room 26?

Aldo spent a long time in our classroom that night, because he brought in stacks of extra chairs and left them in the corner.

"Mrs. Brisbane said she's going to need these tomorrow," he explained.

Why did Mrs. Brisbane need more chairs? Was she going to get more students? If so, wouldn't she need a helpful classroom pet more than ever?

∿

Later, I made a few more notes in my notebook.

Reasons I'm sad about leaving Room 26:
- *Leaving Mrs. Brisbane*
- *Leaving Og*
- *Leaving my new classmates just when I'm starting to like them*

I opened the lock-that-doesn't-lock and strolled over to Og's tank.

"Og, old friend, I think I'm going to be leaving Room Twenty-six," I said. "Even though I don't want to."

Og bounced up and down so hard, I thought he'd pop the top off his tank. "BOING-BOING-BOING!"

"I'm sure you'll still help the students with their problems," I said. "And I'll come visit you every night."

Og calmed down a little then.

"Maybe Mrs. Brisbane will bring another pet in to keep you company. A cold-blooded animal, like you." I thought that would make him feel better, but I don't think it did.

He dived into the water side of his tank, splashing furiously.

I understood.

I went back to my cage, but I didn't sleep much that night.

My last night in Room 26.

HUMPHREY'S RULES OF SCHOOL: Work together. Please!

The Best Class in the World

~•~

I was on edge all morning. Everything in class was running smoothly now, and suddenly the new students of Room 26 didn't seem so strange anymore. Too bad I'd be leaving so soon!

I tried to shake and wiggle my worries away, but this time, it didn't work.

I waited and waited and waited to get the bad news, but nothing happened until after lunch, when Miss Becker came in, accompanied by Richie and Gail. They were smiling, naturally, because they were happy they were getting me back.

"Mrs. Brisbane, your students from last year wanted to share some news with you. Do you have a minute?" Miss Becker asked.

Mrs. Brisbane looked surprised, but she said, "Sure, if you can share the news with my whole class."

Miss Becker smiled. "Yes, of course." She turned toward the class. "Mrs. Brisbane's students from last year wanted to get a classroom pet," she told the class. "Of course, they missed Humphrey and Og. So, I've finally made a decision. Richie and Gail, would you like to announce it?"

"Hermit," Richie said, stepping forward.

That didn't sound like my name at all.

"Crabs," Gail said, giggling.

That didn't sound like Og's name, either.

"What?" Mrs. Brisbane looked amazed.

"We decided on something completely different. Six hermit crabs," Miss Becker said. "It was Ms. Mac's suggestion."

"Wonderful!" Mrs. Brisbane said. "How did you choose them?"

"We decided there would never be a frog as great as Og," Richie said.

"Or a hamster as perfect as Humphrey," Gail added.

I wasn't sure if that was true, but it was nice to hear.

"And," Miss Becker added, "hermit crabs are very quiet. But they do better if they live in groups."

"I hope you enjoy them as much as we enjoy Humphrey and Og," Mrs. Brisbane said. "Perhaps we'll come and visit them someday."

But at the end of the day, before she left, Mrs. Brisbane said, "You notice it takes six hermit crabs to replace the two of you."

That made me feel VERY-VERY-VERY good.

◦⌢◦

"Whew! That was a close call, Og," I told my neighbor when we were alone again.

I was unsqueakably delighted that I'd be staying in

Room 26. After all, someone needed to keep a close eye on Kelsey to make sure she didn't have any accidents. Joey wouldn't get to hear me giggle if I weren't around. Harry's family's clock could be set back at any time. I still wanted to find out why Phoebe was so forgetful, and I wasn't sure yet whether all of Thomas's stories were real or just tall tales.

~•~

I had a second surprise later that afternoon when Ms. Mac appeared at the door.

"Are you ready?" she asked.

"Come on in," Mrs. Brisbane said.

I guess I'd been dozing when Mrs. Brisbane had announced what was going to happen. Suddenly, my classmates were arranging the spare chairs stacked in the corner and setting them next to their own chairs. Then I was SURPRISED-SURPRISED-SURPRISED when Ms. Mac and her entire class of first-graders entered the room.

Ms. Mac directed each of the first-graders to sit next to an older student.

"The idea behind Brisbane's Reading Buddies is that the older children will share their favorite books with the younger children," Mrs. Brisbane told them. "Any questions?"

A small boy who was missing both of his top front teeth raised his hand. "What's over there?" he asked, pointing toward the table Og and I shared.

"Why, that's our hamster, Humphrey, and our frog, Og," Mrs. Brisbane explained.

146

"HI-HI-HI!" I squeaked, which made most of them giggle.

"Maybe you'll be in this class someday and they'll be *your* classroom pets," Mrs. Brisbane said.

That seemed to please the first-graders. It pleased me, too.

What pleased me even more was watching the students in my class patiently sharing books with the first-graders and helping them learn to read.

How on earth could I have ever thought they were the worst class in the world?

～～

The third surprise of the day came just before school was over for the day. Principal Morales stopped by for a visit. He was wearing a tie with colorful autumn leaves on it.

"Class, I just want to say that Mrs. Brisbane has told me that in the last few weeks, your class has improved more than any class she's ever had. Mrs. Brisbane has been teaching for a long time, so that's quite a compliment." Mr. Morales paused and smiled at the class.

"She said you've made special progress in learning to work together," he continued. "So I would like to congratulate you and encourage you to keep up the good work!"

Every face in Room 26 had a smile on it. Even mine.

After school, Mrs. Brisbane hummed to herself as she gathered up her papers and her purse.

"Fellows, this has been quite a week, hasn't it? It's

the kind of week that makes me glad I'm still teaching," she said.

That was nice to hear, because I didn't want Mrs. Brisbane to stop teaching—ever!

"I still have to decide who takes you home this weekend, Humphrey," she said. "It will have to be a surprise."

I didn't mind being surprised. The new students in Room 26, who had seemed like strangers a few weeks ago, all felt like friends now.

That was a very nice feeling.

~·~

When Aldo came into the room that night, the first thing he said was, "Hermit crabs!"

He laughed so hard, his mustache shook. "I never would have guessed she'd pick hermit crabs. They're crustaceans, you know."

"No, I didn't know," I told Aldo. "But it doesn't matter whether they're crustaceans or primates or amphibians—they're classroom pets. And I'll bet they'll do a very good job."

~·~

Of course I couldn't resist the temptation to pay a visit to Room 18 after Aldo's car had pulled out of the parking lot that night.

But as I slid under the door of Miss Becker's classroom, I was a little nervous. What if hermit crabs were as unfriendly as George?

I looked at the table by the windows, but there were only stacks of folders there. An eerie glow from another wall caught my attention and there, on a table, was a large aquarium with a small light on it.

I inched closer and looked up at the unsqueakably odd sight of the hermit crabs. They weren't golden and furry, like me. And they weren't green and googly-eyed like Og. They were pinkish and shiny and had pincers that I wouldn't like to come in contact with. But I have to admit, they were interesting.

"Welcome to Longfellow School," I said, even though they probably couldn't understand me. "I hope you know that you're in one of the best classes in the world."

They just kept wiggling, so I continued. "And I'm in one of the other best classes in the world."

Since they didn't have anything to say, I turned away, but before I left the room, I turned back.

"By the way," I squeaked. "My name is Humphrey. I'm the hamster in Room Twenty-six."

I'm not completely sure, but I think one of the hermit crabs waved to me. I waved back.

∿

Once I was back to my classroom, I told Og about the hermit crabs.

"I guess it's nice that they're all crustaceans," I told him. "But personally, I'd rather have an amphibian as a neighbor. It makes life more interesting."

"BOING-BOING-BOING!" he said, which made me think he was happy to share the table with a rodent.

I took out my little notebook and I finished my poem, writing in the moonlight.

Autumn, oh, autumn,
You had my poor head spinning.
But now I am happy
To have a new beginning!

HUMPHREY'S RULES OF SCHOOL: Love the class you're in.
I do!

Humphrey's Top 10 Rules for Classroom Pets

(hamsters, frogs, and even hermit crabs)

1. Listen to your teacher. If it wasn't for your teacher, you wouldn't have a job and you might still be stuck in a boring old pet store!

2. When a student needs help, always lend a paw. (If you have pincers instead of paws, be VERY-VERY-VERY careful.)

3. If you have a lock-that-doesn't-lock, keep it a secret!

4. Remember: all doors are not the same height, and being stuck under one is unsqueakably scary.

5. In case of emergency (and classroom pets have many of those), try and stay CALM.

6. Learn to tell time. It's a skill that can come in very handy.

7. Be a friend to other classroom pets, even if they're a different species.

8. Even if they seem strange, new students can be every bit as nice as old, familiar students.

9. You can learn a lot about yourself by taking care of another species. (That's what Ms. Mac said, and she's unsqueakably smart.)

10. *Humans need you.* Please be kind to them!

Dear Readers,

I loved summer vacation when I was growing up, but I was also happy when school started again in the fall. I could see all my friends again, and there was the excitement and promise of a new classroom and a new teacher.

Our hamster hero had a great summer at Camp Happy Hollow, but in *School Days According to Humphrey*, he's also happy to be returning to Longfellow School in the fall.

However, there's something human students know that Humphrey doesn't: When they go back to school in the fall, they have a new classroom and teacher.

So when he returns to Room 26, he's unsqueakably surprised—and shocked—to find out that his classmates like Speak-Up-Sayeh and Lower-Your-Voice-A.J. aren't there. Instead, the room is filled with strange students!

At first, Humphrey tries to tell them they're in the wrong room, but his teacher, Mrs. Brisbane, seems happy to see them. Only his fellow classroom pet, Og the frog, seems upset about this mix-up.

Humphrey knows Small-Paul and Slow-Down-Simon from the past. But who are Be-Careful-Kelsey and Just-Joey? Why is the girl called Phoebe so forgetful? And are Thomas T. True's tall tales really true?

This class has so many problems, Humphrey thinks it's the worst class in the world. No wonder he writes in his notebook:

Summer, oh, summer,
With days long and lazy.
Now that you're over,
Things are going crazy!

As the classroom hamster, Humphrey thinks he ought to lend a helping paw. But can a small furry creature help Hurry-Up-Harry, who is always late, get to class on time or help Small-Paul and Tall-Paul like each other?

And why does Helpful-Holly seem like Too-Helpful-Holly when she tries to help Rolling-Rosie?

Rosie has her own problems, especially since she does a dangerous trick called "popping a wheelie" in her wheelchair.

Humphrey's days are BUSY-BUSY-BUSY trying to help these strange students. But evenings are just as demanding because each night, he roams the halls of Longfellow School, searching for clues about what happened to his old friends, who are now in several different classrooms.

And that's not all that Humphrey has to worry about. There's Rockin' Aki, a dancing robot, to deal with and a dangerous encounter with a chiming clock. And he's pretty sure that he and Og are going to be moved to other classrooms—away from Mrs. Brisbane!

It's an exciting start for the school year, but as Humphrey says in his Rules for Classroom Pets: In case of emergency (and classroom pets have many of those), try and stay CALM.

I hope you enjoy reading about the beginning of Humphrey's new school year as much as I enjoyed writing it.

Your friend,

Betty G. Birney

Meet Humphrey!

Everyone's favorite classroom pet!

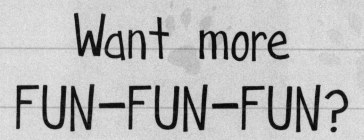

Want more FUN–FUN–FUN?

Find fun Humphrey activities and teachers' guides at www.penguin.com/humphrey.

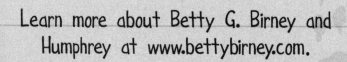

Everyone's favorite classroom pet!

The World according to Humphrey

Betty G. Birney

Welcome to Room 26, Humphrey!

You can learn a lot about life by observing another species. That's what Humphrey was told when he was first brought to Room 26. And boy, is it true! In addition to his classroom escapades, each weekend this amazing hamster gets to sleep over with a different student. Soon Humphrey learns to read, write, and even shoot rubber bands (only in self-defense). Humphrey's life would be perfect, if only the teacher weren't out to get him!

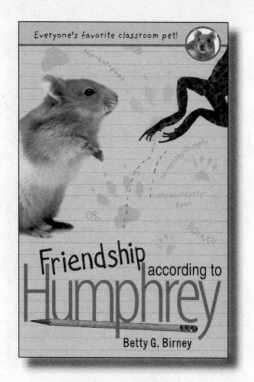

Everyone's favorite classroom pet!

Friendship according to Humphrey

Betty G. Birney

A New Friend?

Room 26 has a new class pet, Og the frog. Humphrey can't wait to be friends with Og, but Og doesn't seem interested. To make matters worse, the students are so fascinated by Og, they almost stop paying attention to Humphrey altogether! Humphrey knows that friendship can be tricky business, but if any hamster can become buddies with a frog, Humphrey can!

Everyone's favorite classroom pet!

Trouble according to Humphrey

Betty G. Birney

Humphrey to the Rescue!

Humphrey the hamster loves to solve problems for his classmates in Room 26, but he never meant to create one! Golden-Miranda, one of his favorite students, gets blamed when Humphrey is caught outside of his cage while she's in charge. Since no one knows about his lock-that-doesn't-lock, he can't exactly squeak up to defend her. Can Humphrey clear Miranda's name without giving up his freedom forever?

Surprises for Humphrey!

A classroom hamster has to be ready for anything, but suddenly there are LOTS-LOTS-LOTS of big surprises in Humphrey's world. Some are exciting, such as a new hamster ball. But some are scary, such as a run-in with a cat and a new janitor who might be from another planet. Even with all that's going on, Humphrey finds time to help his classmates with their problems. But will Mrs. Brisbane's unsqueakable surprise be too much for Humphrey to handle?

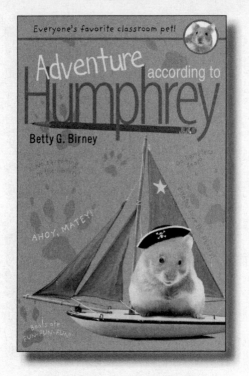

Everyone's favorite classroom pet!

Adventure according to Humphrey

Betty G. Birney

AHOY, MATEY!

Humphrey Sets Sail!

Humphrey's friends in Room 26 are learning about the ocean and boats, and Humphrey can't contain his excitement. He dreams about being a pirate on the high seas; and when the students build miniature boats to sail on Potter's Pond, Humphrey thinks he might get his wish. But trouble with the boats puts Humphrey in a sea of danger. Will Humphrey squeak his way out of the biggest adventure of his life?

Humphrey Is a Happy Camper!

When Humphrey hears that school is ending, he can't believe his ears. What's a classroom hamster to do if there's no more school? It turns out that Mrs. Brisbane has planned something thrilling for Humphrey and Og the frog: they're going to camp with Ms. Mac and lots of the kids from Room 26! Camp is full of FUN-FUN-FUN new experiences, but it's also a little scary. Humphrey is always curious about new adventures, but could camp be too wild even for him?

Everyone's favorite classroom pet!

School Days according to
Humphrey

Betty G. Birney

Roll-Roll-Rolling-Rosie

It's the wrong room!

Rules of school

Hurry-Up-Harry

Pop a wheelie!

Who Are These Kids?!

After an unsqueakably fun summer at camp, Humphrey can't wait to get back to Room 26 and see all of his class-mates. But something fur-raising happens on the first day of school—some kids he's never seen before come into Mrs. Brisbane's room. And she doesn't even tell them they're in the wrong room! While Humphrey gets to know the new students, he wonders about his old friends. Where could they be? What could have hap-pened to them?! It's a big mystery for a small hamster to solve. But as always, Humphrey will find a way!

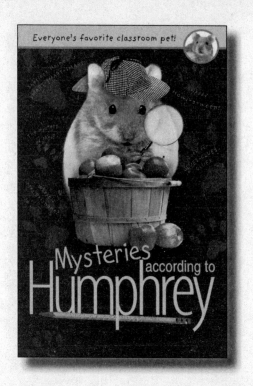

Mysteries according to Humphrey

EEK-EEK-EEK! Mrs. Brisbane Is Missing!

Humphrey has always investigated things, like why Speak-Up-Sayeh was so quiet and Tall-Paul and Small-Paul didn't get along, but this is a true mystery—Mrs. Brisbane is missing! She just didn't show up in Room 26 one morning and no one told Humphrey why. The class has a substitute teacher, called Mr. E., but he's no Mrs. Brisbane. Humphrey has just learned about Sherlock Holmes, so he vows to be just as SMART-SMART-SMART about collecting clues and following leads to solve the mystery of Mrs. Brisbane. . . .

Everyone's favorite classroom pet!

Winter according to Humphrey

Betty G. Birney

A Hamsterific Celebration of the Best Time of the Year!

Room 26 is abuzz. The students are making costumes and practicing their special songs for the Winter Wonderland program, and Humphrey is fascinated by all the ways his classmates celebrate the holidays (especially the yummy food). He also has problems to solve like how to get Do-It-Now-Daniel to stop procrastinating, convince Helpful-Holly to stop stressing over presents, and come up with the perfect gift for Og the frog. Of course he manages to do all that while adding delightful heart and humor to the holiday season.

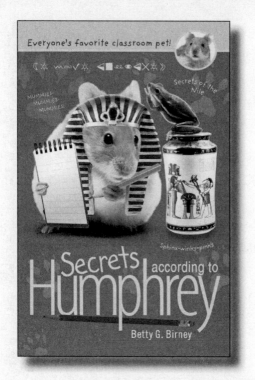

Everyone's favorite classroom pet!

Secrets of the Nile

MUMMIES-MUMMIES-MUMMIES!

Sphinx-winks-pinks

Secrets according to Humphrey

Betty G. Birney

Room 26 Is Full of Secrets, and Humphrey Doesn't Like It One Bit!

So many secrets are flying around Room 26 that Humphrey can barely keep track. Mrs. Brisbane knows a student is leaving, but Humphrey can't figure out which one. (Even more confusing, Mrs. Brisbane seems unsqueakably *happy* about it.) The class is studying the Ancient Egyptians, and some of the kids have made up secret clubs and secret codes. Even Aldo is holding back news from Humphrey.

Humphrey's job as classroom pet is to help his humans solve their problems, but all these secrets are making it HARD-HARD-HARD!

Everyone's favorite classroom pet!

Imagination according to Humphrey

Betty G. Birney

Imagination = excitement

Books can take you anywhere!

Brain blizzard

if a hamster could fly...

Even a Little Hamster Can Have a Big Imagination!

Imaginations are running wild in Mrs. Brisbane's class, but Humphrey is stumped. His friends are writing about where they would go if they could fly, but Humphrey is HAPPY-HAPPY-HAPPY right where he is in Room 26. It's pawsitively easy for Humphrey to picture exciting adventures with dragons and knights in the story Mrs. Brisbane is reading aloud. If only his imagination wouldn't disappear when he tries to write. Luckily, Humphrey likes a challenge, and Mrs. Brisbane has lots of writing tips that do the trick.

WATCH OUT FOR HUMPHREY'S
BOOK OF UNSQUEAKABLY
FUN JOKES AND PUZZLES!

IF YOU LIKE PETS AND ANIMALS,
BE SURE TO PICK UP HUMPHREY'S
BOOK OF PET FACTS AND TIPS!

21982319811356